HOW TO WIN THE WILD BILLIONAIRE

JOSS WOOD

MILLS & BOON

First published in Great Britain 2021
by Mills & Boon, an imprint of HarperCollins*Publishers* Ltd,
1 London Bridge Street, London, SE1 9GF

www.harpercollins.co.uk

HarperCollins*Publishers*
1st Floor, Watermarque Building,
Ringsend Road, Dublin 4, Ireland

Large Print edition 2021

How to Win the Wild Billionaire © 2021 Joss Wood

ISBN: 978-0-263-28885-8

08/21

MIX
Paper from
responsible sources
FSC C007454

This book is produced from independently certified
FSC™ paper to ensure responsible forest management.
For more information visit www.harpercollins.co.uk/green.

Printed and bound in Great Britain
by CPI Group (UK) Ltd, Croydon, CR0 4YY

HOW TO WIN
THE WILD
BILLIONAIRE

CHAPTER ONE

IF YOU GIVE me custody of Olivia, I will forgive your past behavior.

If you don't fight me on this, we can be a family again. You'll be welcomed back into my house, into my life.

Bay Adair pulled up alongside the lavender house in Bo Kaap, two blocks over from Layla and Ali's house—her house now—and lifted her hands off the steering wheel, irritated to see the fine tremor in her fingers. She was shaking. Still. A full day after her ugly confrontation with her father.

He could still, damn him, shake the foundations of her world. And she was furious that, for just a minute, she'd considered his offer, her need to be a part of a family again temporarily overriding logic. But then common sense had kicked in and she'd realized that nothing had changed, that he was just playing her and, worst of all, using Olivia as a tool to bend her to his will.

Her father was an expert in emotional manipulation, Bay reminded herself, and his love was fully conditional.

I will only love you if you do as I say.
I will only love you if you believe what I do.
Well, damn him and damn that!

He'd been playing these games for more than half of her life and Bay was done. He didn't, not really, want custody of Olivia—the fact that neither he nor her mother had tried to see their grandchild in the six months since Layla's death led to that conclusion.

So no, she would not let him use her orphaned niece as a pawn in his twisted game. He wanted control over her, like he had complete control over her mother, and his promise of love and forgiveness was a lure, bait to get her to fall into line. She wasn't stupid enough, weak enough, to believe otherwise.

It was a timely and tough reminder that love always, *always*, came with strings attached.

Bay glanced in the rearview mirror. She frowned when she saw the telltale flush of fever on little Olivia's face. Her big, black eyes normally sparkled with fun and mischief but today, thanks to a vicious cold, they were red-rimmed and flat.

Bay rubbed her fingers across her forehead, hoping to rub away the headache settling behind her eyes. Turning her head, she saw the navy door to the house opening and smiled when she saw Mama B step onto the small landing above the whitewashed steps dressed, as she always was, in a loose, long-sleeved caftan. Today's hijab, her head covering, was a deep, dark purple.

Bay jumped out of the car and jogged up the short flight of stairs to take Mama B's hands in hers. She kissed one wrinkled cheek, then another. "Thanks for taking Olivia. I really appreciate it."

Mama B waved her gratitude away. "She's my great-grandchild—of course I'd help." She frowned. "You said that you think she's coming down with something?"

"I think it's just a cold."

Bay had only been Liv's "mom" for six months and, after years of world traveling and only being responsible for herself, she was still overwhelmed by her new responsibility. What the hell had her younger sister Layla and her husband Ali been thinking when they made her guardian of Olivia? Sure, she could understand why they didn't name her parents—her father's recent behavior hammered that nail home—but Ali had wonderful cousins, any of whom would've been happy to welcome Liv into their ever-expanding broods.

But no, for some crazy reason Layla and Ali decided that Bay, with no child-rearing experience, was the person they wanted to raise their beautiful daughter. And she was beautiful, with her black curls, her creamy, light brown skin reflecting her dad's Cape Malay heritage, pink rosebud mouth and those deep, super-dark eyes. She was also demanding and willful, energetic and mischievous and, yeah, extremely tiring. Being a single mother was tiring.

Being a single mother trying to earn enough to support her and Liv was freaking exhausting.

"Why are you heading to The Vane today?" Mama B asked.

Bay crossed her arms and rocked on her heels. "I'm going to see Digby Tempest-Vane…"

Mama B's drawn-on eyebrows, thin and arched, lifted in surprise. "The Wild Billionaire? Wasn't he the one who had an affair with that opera singer?"

Mama B was confusing Digby with his father, the notorious, rich-as-a-king philanderer who, together with his equally scandalous wife, kept the city, the country—and pretty much the world—entertained when tales of their parties, fights and licentious affairs made front-page news.

"His father, Gil, had the affair with the opera singer, Mama B." But the press did call Digby the Wild Billionaire because of his love of speed, adrenaline and adventure.

He also turned over girlfriends—socialites, models and aristocracy—with the speed of a spinning top. His aversion to commitment, marriage and family was well documented. With parents like his, she couldn't blame him. Neither could she judge him, as Bay had, as soon as she could, left the country and put as many miles between her and her parents as was humanly possible.

Bay saw that Mama B was still waiting for an explanation. "Do you remember Brin? And Abigail, they lived in the house on the corner of my street?"

Mama B nodded.

"Brin is engaged to Radd Tempest-Vane and Abigail works for him. A few weeks ago, Brin told me Digby has been looking for an interior designer for months. He wants to renovate certain rooms of The Vane hotel. Brin is away on holiday with Radd but Abby got me an appointment to meet with Digby."

Bay twisted her lips, not feeling confident about the upcoming meeting. Honestly, she thought it was a waste of her time. And his.

According to Brin, Digby had interviewed various interior designers, the best in the business locally and internationally, but he had yet to find anyone who understood his vision.

Bay didn't think that she, an amateur—she'd received her diploma but never worked as an interior designer—would be the answer to Digby Tempest-Vane's prayers.

But she desperately needed a job and this was her only opportunity to earn money doing something she loved. Her savings were rapidly dwindling and while she'd inherited Layla and Ali's house on their death, they hadn't left much in the way of hard cash.

She was fast running out of funds and if she couldn't find work as an interior designer, she'd have to look for work as an engineer. She'd be miserable but she'd be miserable while earning a lucrative salary.

Ugh. She'd rather stab herself repeatedly in the eye with a rusty fork.

Working for Digby Tempest-Vane would give her wheezing bank account a hit of oxygen. It would also, she presumed, open doors to future interior-design business. But, her voice of reason reminded her, if Morris and Campagno, two famous designers, one based in New York and one in London, couldn't nail the brief, Bay didn't hold out much hope that she could.

But she had to try.

"Trust in yourself, Bay darling, and trust your talent. And if you don't believe in yourself, how can you expect that Tempest-Vane creature to?" Mama B asked, her head tipping to the side.

Bay looked down at their still interlinked hands, one light, one dark, and felt grateful she had this wise woman in her life. Bay was the product of a privileged, superconservative family who lived their lives behind the huge walls of their Rondebosch mansion, carefully choosing the people they interacted with. Rich people, privileged people, white people. Their daughter and granddaughter living in the mostly Muslim, vibrant neighborhood of the Bo Kaap suburb was not acceptable.

Luckily Bay had a lifetime of practice in bucking, fighting against or flat-out ignoring her parents' dictates, opinions and demands. Mama B, sweet, tough and proud, had become, in just half a year, her family, and hers was the only opinion she listened to.

After carrying a now sleeping Olivia into Mama B's house, Bay thanked Mama B again, kissed her cheek and hopped back into her car.

Fifteen minutes later, Bay swung her small car into the oak-lined driveway to The Vane, the ancient branches forming a canopy over the road. Table Mountain, dramatic and ever changing, loomed over the rambling pale green-and-white hotel. The hotel had been, for more than a century, an oasis of calm and elegance in the heart of the city. It was where captains of industry did deals in meeting rooms and bars, where royalty and celebrities chose to lay their heads.

Bay parked her car and looked around. She'd never visited the iconic institution before and she allowed her eyes to drift from the impressive buildings to Table Mountain and back again. *Wow*. The grounds, from the little she could see, were also magnificent, with carefully manicured bright green lawns separating beds of brightly colored flowers and interesting shrubs. If memory served, there was an award-winning rose garden behind the hotel, and she'd read that lovely, whimsical fountains and wrought iron gazebos dotted the extensive grounds.

As with all six-star resorts, there were numerous heated pools, tennis courts, a state-of-the-art gym with private trainers, spas, boutiques and a hair salon.

Luxurious, romantic, iconic...

Again... What was she doing here?

Money, honey.

Bay flipped down her visor to check her appearance. She'd twisted her long, wavy hair into a loose knot at the back of her neck and it looked reasonably okay. She'd slapped some foundation on her face but it, as per normal, hadn't managed to cover the heavy spray of freckles on her nose and high cheekbones. Her whiskey-colored eyes—her best feature in her opinion—reflected her anxiety and general exhaustion.

Bay looked down at her pale pink T-shirt and tailored black pants, which were a little baggy around the butt and thighs. Since returning to Cape Town, she'd lost weight and, as she was naturally slender, they were pounds she couldn't afford to lose.

Right. She was here, best get on with it.

Bay tucked her T-shirt back into her pants and pushed her fist into her sternum. Life had taught her to be a realist and she really didn't think she had an ice cube's chance in hell of being employed by Digby Tempest-Vane as his interior designer.

But, if she didn't try, she'd always have regrets and second-guess herself.

She was allowed to fail. And she probably

would. But failure was only acceptable when she'd given it her best shot.

Digby Tempest-Vane was experiencing a bad-dream hangover. Having had the same recurring nightmare since he was fourteen, he was familiar with its aftereffects of feeling antsy, unsettled and irritated. Sometimes he wouldn't have the dream for months but, whenever he was dealing with change—like now—it was a nightly visitor.

The image of Radd's coffin, plain black like Jack's, being lowered into a deep, black hole jumped onto the big screen of his mind, and he slammed his eyes shut, hoping to force it away. Because he needed to check on his brother, he wouldn't be able to function if he didn't, he pulled his phone out of his pocket and punched in Radd's number.

This is Radd Tempest-Vane. I'm not available at the moment. Leave a message.

Digby disconnected the call, frustrated and irritated at his inability to reach his brother. They were business partners and best friends but for the past few weeks, their relationship ran a very distant second to Radd's romance with Brin.

He was happy for Radd, he *was*, but he couldn't help feeling relegated to the sidelines of his life, pushed aside and well, yeah, forgotten.

Digby, standing at the window of his sprawling office with its amazing view of Table Mountain, placed the palm of his hand on the glass and told himself to stop behaving like a teenage girl. Radd was in love, he was happy and that was all that mattered.

And yeah, if Digby didn't have the same access to him as before, if he was feeling a little lonely and a lot left out—he'd regressed to sounding like a ten-year-old—then that was his problem, not Radd's.

Radd had only fallen in love; he hadn't, like their parents, disappeared from his life. He hadn't, like their elder brother, Jack, *died*. But Digby couldn't help feeling, just a little, abandoned. It was, thanks to being the youngest son of the world's most neglectful parents, an emotion he was very familiar with.

Intellectually he knew he was being stupid, but his heart refused to listen to reason. It was stubborn that way.

But, seriously, if one more person—friend, foe or reporter—asked him whether he'd changed his mind about love and marriage and whether he was going to follow Radd's example and settle down, he'd punch someone or something.

Radd was the only family Digby had, all he needed.

It was his most closely held secret that he lived in constant fear of losing his brother, so why on earth would he want to increase his stress load by having more people in his life to worry about? No, he preferred to fly solo, thank you very much.

Digby sighed and turned away, eyeing his very messy desk. After wrapping up the purchase of the Botswana diamond mine from Vincent Radebe, Radd and Brin decided to take a month-long vacation in the Maldives. That meant Digby taking on Radd's responsibilities to the Tempest-Vane group of companies as well as his own and he was slammed. And stressed.

He should've canceled his meeting with

Brin's interior-designer friend; he really didn't have the time to meet her and he doubted a no-name interior designer would be able to grasp what he wanted when it came to re-decorating The Vane. And until he found a kindred spirit, someone who got his vision for the most favorite of all the Tempest-Vane properties, he'd wait to redecorate and reno-vate.

It wasn't like the wallpaper was falling from the walls or the paint was cracking. The last renovation was completed ten years ago, shortly before he and Radd purchased the hotel, the first business in their quest to restore the Tempest-Vane businesses and as-sets their father sold in order to line his per-sonal pockets.

The hotel still looked good. Great, even.

But he didn't want good or great, he wanted fabulous, unique, a combination of breath-taking elegance and comfort, sophistication and warmth. Their safari operation, Kagiso Ranch, was known to be one of the best safari lodges in the world; he wanted The Vane to be one of the best hotels in the world. They were close but close wasn't quite good enough...

He intended the hotel to become a favorite amongst the world's elite, and his and Radd's fame as two of the world's youngest billionaires didn't hurt. Over the past few years, he'd made numerous changes and now the only outstanding issue was the decor...

Why couldn't he properly convey his vision for the hotel? He was erudite, many called him charming and most called him charismatic. But, despite his ability to converse with paupers and princes, not one of the designers managed to strike the right balance between sophisticated and luxurious but also warm and welcoming. Some of the designs were too cold and too austere, others were too country house.

He didn't think Brin's friend would succeed where the best in the world had failed. He should've just canceled...

Too late now, Digby thought, glancing at his watch. He was due to meet her—God, what was her name again?—in the lobby in five minutes.

Digby buttoned his loose collar as he walked out of his office and pushed up the knot of his tie and straightened his tiepin. Tucking his phone into the inside pocket of his jacket, he ran a hand over his jaw, thanking God stubble was still in fashion.

"Muzi Miya-Mathews wants to know if you have five minutes for him," Monica, his personal assistant, said, looking at him while she continued to type. How the hell did she do that?

Digby nodded and looked around, not seeing his best friend. "He said he'd wait for you on the south veranda but if you don't have time to spare, he'd call you later."

Digby thanked Monica and hurried to the lobby, rapidly moving across the harlequin-tiled floor to the south veranda. He and Muzi had met at Duncan House, one of the best private boys' schools in the country, nearly twenty-five years ago and had been best friends ever since. Except for Radd, nobody knew him better than Muzi Miya-Mathews.

Spotting the dark-skinned Muzi—he was an exceptionally tall, well-built guy so he was hard to miss—Digby hurried over to him and slapped his shoulder. "Three M," he said, using Muzi's nickname from school.

Muzi shook his hand and pulled him into a brief, one-armed hug. "Dig, how's it going?"

"Good. Crazy." Digby shoved his suit jacket back to push his hands into the pockets of his pants. "I've got a meeting in five so I can't hang around. What are you doing here?"

"I'm conducting interviews for a new winemaker for Tangle Vines." Muzi leaned his shoulder into a pillar. Muzi, he remembered, needed a winemaker for his ever-expanding group of wineries.

"If I think the candidate has potential, I'll take them out to the vineyard." Muzi sent Digby a sour look. "Seven interviews and I've yet to make that drive."

Digby sympathized. He knew what it was like not finding the person who gelled, clicked, the person you were looking for.

"Look, I know you are in a hurry but I wanted to tell you that we've made a formal decision to try to purchase Saint Urban. I was wondering if you could put me in contact with the owner."

The Saint Urban vineyard had been his mom's property, and when his parents died two years ago, the vineyard became part of their trust. Neither he nor Radd were beneficiaries of that trust and had no idea who was.

"Sorry, we still don't know who that is," Digby replied. His parents' heir would not only inherit Saint Urban but also Gil and Zia's art and car collection, a couple of huge insurance policies, their extensive property portfolio and a few healthy bank accounts.

He was bitter and he had a right to be. The trust was funded by the sale of Tempest-Vane assets, and the fact that someone unconnected to them was going to reap the rewards of the hard work of generations was a bitter pill to swallow. But Gil and Zia had no sense of family loyalty. If they had, they would've taken a great deal more interest in their three sons.

Digby always knew he was unwanted. His parents paid little to no attention to him, and his achievements, sports and scholastic, went unnoticed. His oldest brother, Jack, had been more of a parent to him than both his parents combined, and his death, shortly before Digby's fifteenth birthday, rocked his already shaky world. Six months, maybe a year later Digby concluded it was better, safer to push people away before they could leave him.

His greatest fear was loving someone again and having them leave, and his recurring dream of Radd dying had him experiencing cold sweats and sleepless nights. He couldn't lose someone else he loved, he wouldn't be able to survive it. So, despite his charm, his wide circle of friends and his popularity, there were only a handful of people he allowed underneath his tungsten-hard suit of armor.

His anxiety was his biggest secret and no one in the world had any idea that the charming, sometimes reckless, wild Digby Tempest-Vane lived with a constant, low-grade fear of being alone, of being abandoned.

Yeah, the press would love that story...

"Anyway, I wanted to give you a heads-up about the offer to purchase Saint Urban," Muzi told him. "Let's grab a beer and catch up sometime."

Digby glanced down at his watch. God, he was late; he needed to hustle. He told Muzi he'd be in touch and, as he walked away from his friend, at the entrance to the still-closed bar, he noticed a flash of cream-and-brown fabric next to an ornate pot holding a miniature palm tree. Digby bent down and picked up a slightly battered, two-toned stuffed animal wearing a T-shirt sporting the slogan I'll Always Hang with You.

Digby looked into its funny, weird little face and saw that the stuffed toy was actually a sloth. Cute. Strange but cute. Someone, presumably its owner, had pulled its short hair on the top of its head into a tiny tail and tied it up with a candy-pink ribbon. So this was a girl sloth then.

"Got yourself a new girlfriend?" Muzi teased, shoulder bumping him as he passed him. "I must say, your taste is improving."

"Bastard," Digby muttered, holding the sloth by one arm. Huh, it actually looked like it had Velcro on its feet and hands, allowing the thing to hang from any tree limb or surface. Clever.

He'd hand this in at the front desk and his concierge would send a text message out to all the child minders asking if any of their charges had lost a stuffed toy. It looked well loved and would be claimed within, he bet, the hour...

Digby looked around, hoping to catch the eye of the concierge but his attention was caught by a woman rushing into the lobby. Her hair was a deep golden brown, pulled back to highlight her pixie face. High, sharp cheekbones, more than a few freckles and a wide, sensuous, luscious mouth made for French kissing. She was tall, slim but busty too, all long legs and arms and frantic energy.

She looked around, obviously harassed. But her eyes were on the floor, looking for all the world like she'd dropped something. Digby looked at the toy in his hand and felt a surge of disappointment. If she was looking for the toy then that meant she was a mom…

Probably married or in a relationship.

But even if she was single, she wasn't someone he'd pursue. He didn't date married women or women with children—too much baggage and drama. But damn, she was gut-wrenchingly beautiful in an understated, quiet way. A confusing combination of sexy and sweet.

As if she sensed his eyes on her, her gaze tracked to him and when she saw the stuffed toy in his hand, her shoulders slumped with relief. He saw her chest rise and fall and the tension in her face ease.

Right, so the creature in his hand was important…

Digby watched as she ducked around a group of French tourists, flashing a smile at an elderly man who stood back to let her pass. She adjusted her tote bag over her shoulder and clasped a leather satchel in her other hand as she approached him, a hesitant look on her face.

"I think you have my sloth." Her voice was deeper than he expected, holding a touch of sexy sandpaper.

"He was trying to sneak into the bar," Digby replied on an easy grin. "I think he has a drinking problem."

Her wide mouth tipped up in a smile and Digby caught a glimpse of neat, even white teeth. "Being the poster child for a deadly sin makes him want to drown his sorrows."

He laughed at her quick comeback. Handing the fluffy toy over, his fingers drifted over hers and electricity raced up his arm. *Wow*. It had been a long, long time since he'd experienced such instant, immediate attraction. Working hard to keep his expression bland, Digby pushed back his jacket and shoved his hands into his pockets.

"Do you normally carry alcoholic animals around with you?" he asked.

She looked at the creature and pulled its Velcro legs apart before slapping them together again. "Ah, no. I was a little early and took a walk outside—he must've fallen out of my bag along the way. Thank God you found him or else I would never be forgiven. Mr. Fluffy is an important member of our household."

"Boy or girl?" Digby asked, thinking that he should walk away, that there was no point in drawing out this conversation. Even if she wasn't in a relationship—and of course she would be—he never had affairs with women with kids.

He liked women who could be spontaneous, who could meet him at ten at night for a late drink or at six in the morning for an early run on the beach, who could leave for a weekend away at a moment's notice or answer the door dressed naked.

Digby worked hard and played harder and liked being the sole focus of a woman's attention. That never happened with someone who had kids.

"Ah, a girl. Olivia… Livvie. She's three and she's besotted with this sloth. She's probably throwing a hissy fit of epic proportions because he's missing."

He saw the worry in her eyes, the flash of panic. He instantly, and strangely, wanted to reassure her. Not that he knew what to say. And that was weird too. He could always think of a quick comment. He could bullshit with the best of them.

But not today. And not, he realized, with her.

Digby saw his most senior concierge rapidly crossing the floor to them and sighed. They were about to be interrupted and he wanted more time with this woman, whoever she was. But time was something he didn't have, he was running so late as it was.

"May I be of assistance, sir?" Benoit said, raising his nose as he looked at the woman and the toy in her hand. Benoit could size up the guests in a flash by their clothing, accessories and attitude, and he was never wrong.

Her plain black trousers and equally plain,

light pink T-shirt were clearly off-the-rack and her shoes were scuffed at the toe. Her hair was completely natural and it was obvious she hadn't spent more than five minutes on her makeup.

But she was more lovely than most of the models, actresses and socialites he'd met.

"If you'll accompany me, miss, I'll see if I can be of assistance," Benoit said, looking down his long, aristocratic nose at her.

Digby saw annoyance flash in the woman's eyes and couldn't blame her; Benoit was a hell of a snob. But his stupendously wealthy guests loved the snooty, almost rude concierge, and receiving his deference and approval was something they all aspired to. If you passed muster with Benoit, then you were worthy of your status, your wealth, your place in the world.

It was a ridiculous notion, but Benoit's name was dropped with alarming frequency in the rarefied world he operated in.

Benoit, no last name needed, *arranged a hot-air balloon ride over the wine lands.*

Benoit found me a bottle of Petrus 1990...

Benoit arranged for me to have my portrait painted by Kendall...

Digby didn't particularly like Benoit, but his guests did and that was all that mattered. It would be easy for him to hand her over to Benoit to deal with but, for some strange reason, he wanted to protect her from Benoit's always polite but silently scathing attitude.

"I'll handle it, thank you, Benoit," Digby told him, his tone suggesting that he not argue. Benoit hesitated then nodded, bowing slightly before retreating.

When Benoit was out of earshot, he connected with those cognac-colored eyes again— did his heart really skip a beat or was that his imagination?—and the question he'd been about to ask flew out of his head. He felt the insane urge to find out whether her skin was as soft as it looked.

"I'm Digby Tempest-Vane, by the way."

"My name is Bay Adair."

Bay Adair. The unusual name suited her. What didn't suit him was his fiery, instant, almost out-of-control need to make her his. Again, super strange.

"Are you here to meet someone?"

Irritation flickered in her eyes. "I'm here to meet you, to talk to you about redesigning this hotel."

Hell. Brin's friend. She was here on business, to try to nail a design concept that had eluded ten of the world's best designers.

"Right."

On the plus side, he'd be wasting an hour, maybe two of his time because there was no way Bay would be able to give him what he needed, not in a business sense. Physically, sexually, he had no doubt that she could rock his world.

Life was messing with him by sending him stupid dreams and placing women in his path he couldn't have.

Good thing he had practice at looking it in the eye and telling it to go to hell.

CHAPTER TWO

BAY STRUGGLED TO keep up with Digby Tempest-Vane's long stride as she followed him across the lobby—funny how a space so beautiful and luxurious could still be so cold—toward a set of doors discreetly marked as Staff Only.

Liv's sloth was back in her tote bag and Bay clutched her art satchel to her chest and found herself almost jogging to keep up with him. He was tall, six-two or -three, and his stride was long and brisk. His shoulders were wide, and his short-at-the-sides and raked-back-on-top hair, a deep, rich brown. His eyes, as she'd noticed earlier, were the deep, intense shade commonly used in mosques from Marrakech to Medina, all across the Middle East and North Africa.

Persian blue and brilliant.

She liked his strong jawline under three-day stubble, his straight nose and his sensual mouth. He was panty-dropping attractive, successful and rich. Alpha to the core.

Bay watched as he keyed in a code to open the door leading to the back rooms of the hotel. She'd seen the flicker of annoyance in his eyes and heard his sigh when she told him she was there to see him, and it was obvious he thought meeting her was a waste of his time.

And she couldn't blame him for being skeptical; if the best in the business hadn't been able to nail his vision, then there was little chance she would succeed where they failed. She was, after all, a realist.

When she heard his *Thanks, but no thanks* she could put aside this silly dream of supporting herself and Liv through interior design, and she'd resign herself to living in the real world, the *mundane* world.

After Digby turned her down, she would call Busi Sithebe, of Kane, Sithebe and Pritchard, Consulting Engineers; Busi was her best friend from school and, a year or so ago, she'd told her that when she was ready to return to engineering, she'd try to find a position for her in her company. Bay felt her stomach lurch at the thought of joining the corporate world and working in a field that bored her to tears.

But she was out of options. A girl, and her niece, needed to eat.

It was unbelievable how much could change in a scant six months. Her life—and Liv's obviously—had been flipped upside down and inside out. She lost her sister, and her niece lost her mom and dad...

A picture of their little family—Ali, black eyes flashing, his arm around his pale, blonde wife, and Liv between them, her daddy's child through and through—flashed in front of her eyes and Bay swallowed, blinking to clear her suddenly burning eyes.

She'd been in Goa when she heard the news of their deaths and it had taken her two days to get home. Bay mourned her sister, she *did*, but she'd had to put aside her grief to look after a confused three-year-old who'd had her life ripped apart. She'd initially been in a state of shock on hearing that she'd been appointed as Olivia's legal guardian but that shock soon receded as the enormity of her responsibilities dawned on her.

She was twenty-eight years old and for the past five years, she'd been responsible only for feeding, clothing and looking after herself. Now she had a three-year-old and thoughts of how she was going to pay for Olivia's education, any medical bills, food and clothing kept her awake at night.

Today was D-Day, her very last, almost impossible chance to earn money doing something she loved. If she failed, Bay would have to look for a *proper* job. She sighed at the thought of discussing working hours, remuneration, health insurance and responsibilities.

Honestly, it didn't matter where she found work, whether it was here or somewhere else. Life would change for them and would bring a new set of challenges. She'd have to find daycare for Olivia, dropping her off early and picking her up late. Liv, thanks to losing both her parents, had separation anxiety, and Mama B was the only person, apart from Bay, with whom she felt comfortable. If she went back to work—and she had no choice about that—would Olivia feel abandoned, unloved and rejected? All over again?

But a salary would mean food on the table, money in the bank, a cushion in case of disaster—

"Ms. Adair, I don't have all day."

Digby's cool voice had her jumping back into the present and she noticed that he held a door open for her, waiting for her to step into his office. Bay walked into the expansive and luxurious space and, once inside, turned to watch him shut the door behind him. He immediately shrugged off his tailored suit jacket and loosened his tie. He tossed his jacket over the back of a couch and gestured her to one of the visitor's chairs next to his desk.

"Take a seat," he told her, walking around his huge desk, and dropping into his leather office chair. Almost immediately, he raised his left arm and pushed his hand down the back of his neck in what looked to be an oft-repeated stretch.

Bay watched as the fine cotton of his shirt tightened across that football-field-wide chest and big biceps. He switched hands, elongated his spine, and all the moisture in her mouth dried up.

Digby Tempest-Vane had one of the best bodies she'd ever seen. No contest.

Digby lowered his arms and shrugged. "Sorry, I slept in a weird position last night and my shoulders are tight."

Bay nodded, not wanting to think about Digby in bed. Had he been alone? Did he sleep naked? How big, exactly, was his bed?

Adair! Really?

Digby linked his hands on his flat stomach and Bay couldn't help wondering whether that fine material covered a six-pack. She was damn sure it did...

Digby's eyes—that intense blue—rested on her face and Bay wondered if he'd bring that same intensity to the way he kissed.

Or made love.

She wasn't someone who spent a lot of time wondering about men and their kisses. She'd had a couple of relationships at the university but, for the past few years, she'd lived her life on her own terms, without reference to anyone else. There had been that guy in Berlin, another in Tasmania, but neither tempted her to stay in one place, to stop traveling. To take a risk with her heart, already decimated by her dad.

She was cautious…extremely cautious.

But she couldn't stop imagining what Digby would look like…well, naked.

Aargh! Resisting the urge to bury her face in her hands, Bay hoped she wasn't blushing, so she looked away and forced herself to change the subject.

"Why don't you just tell me your vision of The Vane and I'll take notes?" Bay suggested, proud of her strong, clear voice. Yeah, a lifetime of hiding her emotions from her parents came in handy sometimes.

Digby reached for a folder on his desk and handed it over. "Here are all the dimensions and a set of photos of all the rooms. You can look at it later."

Bay nodded and tucked the folder into the back of her sketch pad. Digby pushed his chair back and placed his ankle on his knee. "I want restful but sophisticated, comfortable but elegant. Do not give me country house, minimalism or avant-garde…"

Bay's hand dashed across the page, making notes as he spoke, idly noticing that he was doing a great job of telling her what he didn't want but not what he did.

"In the first stage on the revamp, because we can't do everything at once, I want the ballroom, a second honeymoon suite and the coffee shop refreshed. The next-steps phase of the project will be the conference rooms, the lobby and all the other public rooms. The third stage will be the bedrooms. I want the same designer working on all three phases, to keep the vision consistent. I'm imagining that this will be a multiyear project and the designer would need to commit to all three phases. After I sign off on the design, the designer would then take over, using their capital to run the project. I'd be happy to consider paying a deposit but I'd expect my designer to purchase all the supplies, furniture, art and accessories and pay the work crews. I'd then issue payment once the work is completed to my satisfaction."

Digby tossed out his sentences in a flat monotone and it was obvious that he'd repeated these words many times before. Bay felt all hope of securing this project fade away on hearing how Digby planned to structure the deal.

The project was massive, much bigger than she thought, and she couldn't take it on. Oh, there was scope to make a lot of money but she'd have to spend money to make money.

She didn't have that sort of cash available. And, without any security or bank credit—the downfall of traveling the world and not having a credit history—she wouldn't qualify for a small loan, never mind the millions she'd need to see the first stage of this project through.

She didn't have the funds to decorate a doll's house, never mind the city's most exclusive hotel.

Bay closed her sketch pad and leaned back in her chair. "Let's not beat around the bush, Mr. Tempest-Vane—"

"Call me Digby," he suggested.

"It's an exciting project but I'm not the person you are looking for. I don't have the experience for a project this big and even if I did, I don't have the finances to take on something of this magnitude." Bay stood up and shrugged. "So, I'm going to stop wasting your time and let you get back to work."

Digby stared at her for a long minute before climbing to his feet. "I respect your honesty—thank you."

"And now you can tell Brin that you did as she asked and met with me." Brin had sent her a couple of messages asking for an update and she was convinced her friend was harassing Digby, as well.

Digby handed her a wry grin. "She keeps texting me, asking if we've met. I can now tell her we have."

Thanks for trying, Brin.

Bay expected him to bid her a brisk goodbye but, instead of showing her the door, he walked around the desk to pick up his jacket. "Would you like to see the rooms, anyway? I've got some time before my next meeting and I'd like to stretch my legs."

Bay bit her lip, knowing that she should leave, that Liv was probably screaming blue murder because she couldn't find Fluffy the sloth.

But Bay hadn't had a minute off in six months and she hadn't had a proper conversation with an adult, never mind a sexy man, for as long. And, yes please, she really wanted to see more of this iconic hotel.

And, more worrying, she really, really, *really* wanted to spend a little more time with Cape Town's sexiest playboy. He was, after all, eye candy.

After today, she'd never see him again, but for an hour, maybe a little more, she could pretend that she wasn't a struggling single mom dealing with her manipulative father, as well as being almost broke and pretty much at the end of her tether. For a tiny sliver of time, she could go back to being Bay, to being the carefree person she was before the world changed.

He should've just ushered her out of his office and carried on with his day. Showing her the ballroom was a complete waste of time, Digby thought, ushering Bay into an elevator that would take them to the third floor and the grand ballroom.

But he was reluctant to bring their meeting to an end, to see her walk out of his life.

Why? He didn't have a clue.

Maybe it was because she was unlike anyone he'd ever met before. Quiet but not a pushover, polite but direct.

She also seemed very unimpressed by him, which was, frankly, a novelty. Most women he met instantly turned on the charm, played with their hair, batted their eyelashes. With Radd off the market, Digby knew that he was the most eligible bachelor in the country. Not because he was anyone special but because he was a Tempest-Vane, had a fat bank account, an okay-ish face and a fit body.

Women craved his attention because of his name and his wealth and his status, because he had a wild streak and a reputation for being a bit of a bad boy.

They wanted to be the one to tame him, to make him settle down. They were all on a fool's errand. He'd never give a woman that much power over his heart and his life. Losing Jack had nearly destroyed him; he was terrified of losing Radd, and he'd never, ever love someone enough to be constantly worried about whether they lived or died.

Bay Adair was just another in a long line of women he was attracted to, somewhat different, a little mysterious. Her fantastic eyes were unreadable and her expression remained cool and impassive. She was the most self-contained woman he'd ever met and, yeah, he was intrigued. And attracted.

And the longer he stayed in her company, the more he noticed. Her eyebrows were arched and S-shaped, a couple of shades deeper than her shot-with-auburn brown hair. Her mouth was uneven, with a thin top lip and full bottom lip, turning the lopsided feature indescribably sexy. She had a long neck and while she was on the skinny side of slim, she had a round, high butt and amazing breasts.

Her fringe covered her forehead and he wondered how long her hair was, unable to tell because it was wound into a messy bun at the back of her head. Freckles covered her nose and her high cheekbones and, he imagined, her shoulders and back, anywhere the sun touched.

She was ethereal and quirky, nothing like the sharp, sexy, successful women he normally dated. Although dating implied that feelings were involved. His had never been engaged and never would be. And the women he dated, slept with, knew not to expect more from him than a few dates and a good time… it was all he could give.

Relationships required taking a risk and while he'd risk his body—and had many, many times—he'd never risk his heart. That was a step, or hundred, too far.

Uncomfortable with where his thoughts were headed, Digby watched as the elevator doors opened onto the small lobby outside the ballroom and gestured for Bay to walk ahead of him. His eyes flickered to her ass again—gorgeous!—and he sighed when he felt the action in his pants. Time to switch gears, Tempest-Vane.

Bay hurried across the lobby to the closed doors of the ballroom. After grabbing the brass handles, she flung the doors open and stepped into the huge, light-filled space. Walking across the parquet flooring, she then stood in the middle of the room, where so many brides had danced in the arms of their new husbands, slowly turning around, her arms akimbo.

Digby sucked in a breath as an image started to form behind his eyes… Bay wearing a simple, classic wedding dress, fresh flowers in her hair and a broad smile on her face. Her eyes, light and filled with love, were on a man across the room and Digby, unable to help himself, looked in that direction...

But all he saw was an empty room, chairs stacked up against its cream-colored walls.

He rubbed his jaw, thinking that was incredibly weird. And unsettling. He was the type of guy who imagined what women looked like naked, not how they'd look in a bridal gown. This had been a superbly strange day...

"Mmm. The room is very neutral and a little bland," Bay stated, her voice a little raspy. "Neutral, but..."

"Boring?"

"Yeah, boring." Bay nibbled her full luscious bottom lip, and he wanted, very badly, to know whether it tasted as good as it looked. But she hadn't given him a hint that his attraction was reciprocated so no moves, dammit, would be made.

So sad, too bad.

"The light is incredible and the proportions fantastic," Bay said, her light, bright eyes darting everywhere.

Digby tried to see the space through her eyes and admitted it was. It was a double-volume room with crowned ceilings and floor-to-ceiling windows and a highly polished wooden floor. His parents had been married in this room and he'd watched the video of their expensive wedding. His mother looking sensational wearing a Chanel gown, his father in a black topcoat and tails, his face alight with laughter.

Three months after their wedding, his father took over as CEO of Tempest-Vane Holdings and started looting the company. By the time Digby was a teenager, twenty or so years after that society wedding, there was nothing of the family fortune left and the Tempest-Vane holding company was declared insolvent.

There had been no remorse about transferring the company's wealth to their individual bank accounts and, ultimately, to a trust, and their desire to live harder, faster, crazier lives in the pursuit of pleasure simply increased.

Man, they'd been useless parents in every possible way.

No wonder he was emotionally stunted.

Bay cleared her throat and tipped her head to the side. "You don't like this room," she commented.

He liked the room just fine, it was the memories he hated.

Needing air, Digby walked over to the floor-to-ceiling French doors and quickly unlocked them, sliding them against the wall. He walked onto the expansive balcony and gripped the balustrade, looking down onto the rose garden first established by his great-great-grandmother. He smelled Bay's perfume, subtle but sexy, as she joined him and he noticed that her head just reached the top of his shoulder.

He wondered how well she'd fit into his arms...

Bay looked down and gasped. In the garden below them, white roses slid into pink roses, then red, then scarlet. It was, he admitted, a hell of a sight and best seen from up above.

"Mama B would love this," Bay said, resting her forearms on the railing, her eyes dancing over the rose garden.

"Who is that?" Digby asked, turning to lean his hip against the railing.

Bay's smile was soft and gentle. "Mama B is Bella Samsodien, my late sister's grandmother-in-law. The owner of the sloth, Livvie, is her great-granddaughter." Bay darted him a quick look, as if deciding how much to tell him. Then she shrugged quickly and continued.

"My sister and her husband died in a car crash six months ago and they named me as Olivia's guardian."

It took Digby a minute to make sense of her words, to understand that she was raising her sister's child. Intellectually he knew that her actions weren't that out of the ordinary, but since he was a product of parents who hadn't shown any interest in raising their *own* sons, her unselfish action amazed him.

Digby looked at her profile and saw the tension in her mouth, in the cords of her neck. He knew what it felt like to lose a sibling. "I'm sorry. I lost my brother too and I know how hard it is."

Bay nodded. "I miss her, but I'm lucky to have Liv. She's the most amazing little girl."

Digby, who had no experience of children, and didn't want any, didn't know how to respond to that statement.

"Having Olivia in our lives is such a blessing, and Mama B adores her. Ali, my brother-in-law, was Mama B's grandson—she raised him from a baby because her daughter died in childbirth." Sadness flitted across her face. "She's endured so much loss—I don't know how she goes on."

You plow on because you have no damn choice. As he damn well knew. "And you are fond of her." That much was obvious; he saw her face soften every time she mentioned the older lady.

"She's amazing," Bay told him, turning to look at him, her expression earnest. "I was overseas when I heard about the accident. I returned to Cape Town immediately, only to find out that I'd inherited their house and was named Liv's guardian. I was reeling, trying to deal with Layla's death and trying to wrap my head around the fact that I had a child to care for. I knew nothing about children, wasn't even remotely interested in them."

Bay dug into her bag and pulled out her phone, swiping her thumb across the screen. She held it up. "This is Olivia."

Cute, Digby thought. Olivia sported a head of wild dark curls. With her massive round black eyes, rosebud mouth and lovely brown skin, she was the definition of gorgeous.

"We stayed with Mama B for three months, and Liv and I moved out three months ago."

Digby wanted to ask her about her parents, wondering why she hadn't mentioned them, but he could visibly see her retreating. It was obvious that she thought that she'd been too open, shared too much. But he wanted to know more and that was dangerous. He wouldn't be seeing her again...

Pity.

Digby watched as her spine straightened. She pushed her shoulders back and lifted her chin, and their very brief moment of connection wafted away on the slight breeze blowing off Table Mountain.

He shouldn't feel so disappointed; she was just another woman passing through his life.

Yeah, he was attracted to her, found her unusual and unsettling, but he was attracted to women all the time. The days when he chased down everyone who caught his eye were long gone...

"I should get going," Bay said, tucking her hair behind her ears. "I'm sure Olivia is awake, and you have work of your own to do."

She had no idea of the length of his to-do list but meeting Bay was worth having to work late to catch up on lost time today. She was a breath of fresh air. "I do. But before you go, I have something else I want to show you."

Bay frowned. "Another room?"

"No, this can never be redecorated or improved on," Digby said, walking down the balcony. At the corner of the building, where the balcony made a right-angle turn, he stood back and gestured Bay to walk around the corner. She sent him a puzzled look but did as he asked and her sharp intake of breath was what he'd been waiting for.

Joining her at the railing, he smiled at the

incredible view of Table Mountain looming over the hotel. His forefathers had purchased this plot of land purely for the view of the mountain, and it was said to be the best view of the world-famous landmark in the city. Rising above them to an impressive height, it was frequently covered when a rolling cloud, also known as the tablecloth, formed when the southeaster blew. But today the mountain was bare and utterly impressive.

"It's so beautiful. You're so lucky to live here, to have this view," Bay told him, her voice soft with awe and appreciation.

"Standing here on this balcony and look-ing at the mountain is my very first memory," Digby told her, unsure why he was revealing something so personal. "When my brother and I decided to rebuild the Tempest-Vane group of companies, I insisted that this hotel should be the first business we wrestled back."

A smile touched Bay's lovely mouth. "And was it a wrestle?"

He shrugged. "We made the owner an offer

he couldn't refuse. He didn't so it was reasonably easy.

"Unlike the bloody mine," he added, wondering why he was running his mouth. "Now that was a nightmare."

"There's a story there," Bay said, sounding curious.

"Complete with a slightly crazy, utterly demanding bride, my brother meeting Brin, him falling in love and tough negotiations with a greedy mine owner."

Bay smiled, a proper, wide, open smile and Digby placed his hand on the balustrade to anchor himself. Holy hell, that smile was definitely her superpower.

He stared at her, she stared back and he couldn't help his eyes going to her lips, wondering whether her mouth would taste like sunshine. Would her eyes lighten or darken with passion? Would her long fingers slide up his neck, into his hair?

He couldn't let her leave without finding out.

He lowered his mouth, bridging the gap between them. Her lips formed a small "oh"—excitement or surprise?—and because she didn't pull or push him away, he covered her lips with his, lifting his hand to trace his thumb across her cheekbone. Yeah, soft. So soft.

Her mouth was land he wanted to explore, tempting and luscious, but Digby knew he couldn't push; if he did, she'd bolt. He carefully placed his hands on her tiny waist and gently pulled her into him, surprised at how well their bodies fit. Feeling her tension, he ran a reassuring hand down her back and increased the pressure on her mouth, teasing her lips to open, and when she allowed him in, his world—normally so steady—tilted off its axis. Digby felt like he'd taken a hit of something illicit. He felt shaky and disorientated, hot and cold...weird.

He wanted to shake his head to clear it, but that meant dislodging his mouth from Bay's and that was impossible. He'd find the willpower to stop ravaging her mouth, but he'd need a minute more. Or ten.

Bay softened, released a small noise of approval and then those hands were in his hair, running down his neck, across his shoulder blades. She felt like warmth and home and comfort, emotions he didn't normally associate with foreplay.

And this *was* foreplay.

Digby lifted his hand to her shirt, sighing when his hand covered her breast, pleased when her responsive nipple pushed into the palm of his hand. He rubbed his knuckle over the tight point and that action broke the connection between them. Bay jerked back, looking up at him with wide, startled eyes.

"What are we doing?" she whipped the question out, looking as unsettled as he felt.

Digby hoped she wouldn't notice his bobbing Adam's apple and the slight tremor in his hands. "Kissing in the sunlight," he answered, resorting to flippancy.

Bay pushed her hands into her hair, loosening the knot on the back of her head, and Digby watched, fascinated when tendrils fell down her back. He'd love to pull those pins from her hair, to see the contrast between her dark hair, shot with red, and her pale skin, to see where else he could find freckles on her.

"I need to go," Bay said, bending down to pick up her bag and art satchel. He'd been so entranced by her, having her in his arms, he hadn't noticed that she'd dropped either.

He had so much work to do, a meeting to attend, but all Digby wanted to do was to keep kissing her in the summer sun. He knew this property inside out and, following a series of seldom-used corridors, he could walk them through the hotel unseen. They could be in his house at the back of the property in ten minutes; he could have her naked in eleven.

Why this woman and why now? Sex, finding it and enjoying it, was easy. He had at least a dozen women whom he could text and set up dinner, followed by some bed-based fun. Or he could go to a club and pick up a woman, or even, if he was feeling lazy, a guest sitting in his world-famous bar downstairs.

But Bay Adair, Digby realized, was most definitely not easy, in any sense of the word. She wouldn't, he knew, indulge in sex for sex's sake.

Bay sent him a quick, embarrassed smile. "I really hope you find a designer who'll do this place justice. Please don't let them take their inspiration from the decor in the lobby."

"What's wrong with the lobby?" Digby asked. He rather liked the look of the lobby.

Bay wrinkled her nose. "It's cold. It reminds me of a snooty museum or art gallery."

Well, he'd asked. Digby felt Bay's hand on his forearm as she stood on her tiptoes to kiss his cheek. "Thanks for your time. Don't bother seeing me out—I'll find my way."

She moved her lips to his mouth, tasting him quickly before pulling back. "Have a good life, Digby Tempest-Vane."

Digby, still trying to catch up, stared at her slim back as she walked away, wondering how one kiss—admittedly a stunning, earth-shaking, volcanic kiss—could make him feel so shaken, so utterly off balance.

But it had and he was. He didn't, he silently admitted as he gripped the railing with both hands, like either sensation.

CHAPTER THREE

BAY WALKED OUT of the ballroom, caught the elevator to the lobby and ducked into the first ladies' bathroom she came across, grateful to find it empty.

Gripping the basin with both hands, she stared at her reflection, wincing at her flushed cheeks and bright eyes. Her lips looked swollen and red, and anyone with any observational powers would immediately know she'd been thoroughly kissed.

It had been a lot of fun, Bay thought, touching her lips with her fingertips. In the space of a few minutes, Digby turned her to liquid wax and she'd lost track of where she was...

And *who* she was.

Bay hadn't had many lovers—okay, a grand total of two—but she'd kissed enough guys to know that Digby Tempest-Vane had a master's degree in the art of smooching. It had been, by an African mile, the best kiss of her life.

And, probably, her last. For a long, long while.

Pity.

Pulling her thoughts off his expert lips and exceptional body, Bay splashed some water on her hot face and told herself to pull it together. Staring at her reflection in the mirror, she touched her lips, her thoughts returning to how wonderful it felt standing in his arms. She'd felt secure and protected, emotions she hadn't experienced in a long, long time.

Was that why his kiss rocked her off her feet? She'd been completely on her own for five years but, since she was a young teen, she'd been on the outside of her family looking in, on unstable emotional ground. Had she responded like a wild woman to Digby because he was tall and strong, the ultimate alpha male, somebody bigger and stronger than her? Because she'd needed to feel safe?

Was she doing that age-old, biological thing, looking for a strong protector, someone to slay her dragons for her? And if she was, then she was being a complete moron.

She was a strong, independent woman who could, and would, wield her own sword, thank you very much. Relationships—and love—were a quid pro quo, a trade-off, the price always too high to pay.

As she'd suspected, working for Tempest-Vane was an impossibility. She'd taken her shot, missed the basket and it was time to move on. She had a little girl relying on her and she wouldn't let her down.

Pulling her phone from her bag, and ignoring her hollow heart and dread, Bay called Busi's cell. When it went straight to voice mail, Bay called Busi's office. The receptionist told her that Busi was away from her desk and would be unavailable for the next few days. Would she care to leave a message?

Bay left her details and heard the beep of an incoming call. Switching calls, and frowning at the strange number, she stated her name.

"Ms. Adair, my name is Bradbury, and I'm a lawyer representing your parents."

Okay. So why was he calling her?

"This is a courtesy call to inform you that your parents intend to sue for custody of one Olivia Jane Samsodien..."

For the second time in the space of an hour, Bay felt her head swim. Bay caught a glance of herself—her face deathly pale and her lips now bloodless—as she dropped into the wingback chair, thankful it was there because her knees no longer seemed to be working.

This couldn't be happening...

When the first wave of denial and shock passed, Bay rested her forearms on her thighs, staring down at the plush carpet beneath her shoes, and did some deep-breathing exercises. When she felt her panic receding, she pushed her emotions back and forced herself to think. Almost immediately, two thoughts became crystal clear.

First, she needed a lawyer who specialized in family law.

And, second, there was no way she'd allow her rigid, demanding, emotionally crippled parents to raise Layla and Ali's wonderful child.

Unbidden, the memories rolled in, tipped with acid. For the first thirteen years of her life, she'd been her father's model child, happily echoing his macho beliefs about patriarchy and protection. Charismatic and charming, his were the viewpoints she embraced, whether it was on religion, on feminism or on politics.

Then she went away to boarding school and met Busi, her sister of the soul. She'd asked her parents whether Busi could spend the weekend at her house and her parents refused, not giving her a reason for saying no. After badgering them, her father finally snapped, telling her that Busi wasn't like them and that they didn't want her kind in their house.

Her *kind*? Someone sweet and thoughtful and seriously smart? It finally dawned on her that her father's sole objection was to the color of Busi's skin.

Furious, she'd started questioning their racist and misogynistic beliefs and challenging the status quo. She and her father argued about race and religion, feminism and misogyny, and when she refused to back down from a point—or change her mind—he started to withdraw his approval and his demeanor grew cooler.

Then he started to blatantly ignore her and then, to punish her further, turned all his attention, affection and love onto her older sister, Jane, and younger sister, Layla, leaving her to waft in the wind, feeling unsure and abandoned. She lived in their house but her presence was simply tolerated. The only thing that she and her parents agreed on was that they all couldn't wait for her to leave home.

Bay had fought for her freedom, for the right to live her life on her own terms, and she'd never allow Liv to be raised in what she now realized was a toxic environment.

And she'd never allow herself to love someone because it was better to not taste, touch and feel love than to have it and then lose it.

Bay shook her head, conscious of her tight throat and the concrete block resting on her chest.

Her father had tried to bully her into giving him custody of Liv yesterday but when she refused, he'd approached a lawyer and instructed him to sue. He didn't want Liv... he just didn't like hearing the word no.

But, because he and her mother were wealthy, established, charming and personable, and had raised three girls of their own, there was a good chance of them winning.

It didn't help that Bay had no child-rearing

experience, was currently unemployed and was, mostly, living off her savings.

Bay found a tube of lipstick in her bag. She removed the lid and carefully...oh, so carefully, since her hand was shaking...slicked on the pale, taupe color.

She needed work, something to show the courts that she could look after Olivia, that she was the best person for the job. She would not allow her niece to grow up in an environment that stifled creativity, individual thought, that promoted intolerance and didn't celebrate individualism. She wanted Olivia to grow up in a home where she was free to be herself, to explore ideas and faiths and to make up her own mind about what she did and didn't believe in.

She wanted Olivia to know that she was strong, that she was capable and that she would always, always be loved.

Bay would make very sure Olivia knew that her love wasn't conditional.

Digby far preferred Cape Town in summer; he wasn't a fan of short days, wind and rain. In summer, the long, hot days stretched on endlessly. Not that he'd seen a lot of sun lately since he spent most of his time in either of his two offices, the one at The Vane or at the headquarters of Tempest-Vane Holdings.

Digby loosely held the wheel of his Maserati Levante Trofeo, the luxury SUV he bought himself a few months back to celebrate his thirty-fifth birthday, enjoying its growly engine, its great handling and luxury finishes. He glanced down at the fluffy toy on his passenger seat and reached across to rub the nubby fabric between his finger and thumb.

He was on the way to the Bo Kaap neighborhood of Cape Town to deliver Fluffy, the sloth and ultimate escape artist, back to Bay Adair.

After Bay left, he'd walked into another meeting and when that was done, he told Monica he wasn't to be disturbed and immersed himself in work, ignoring his cell and emails as he attempted to whittle down his insane to-do list. When he finally surfaced, it was after seven and he heard a frantic message from Bay Adair on his company voice mail. Bay asked him to please retrace their steps because she'd lost the damn sloth again.

Hearing the exhaustion in her voice, and a trace of panic, he did as she asked and found the stuffed toy lying on the balcony where they exchanged their hot-as-fire kiss.

Digby twisted his lips, feeling like a total ass for not sending one of his many drivers, interns or underlings to deliver the toy. He didn't need to play the role of the courier but he did want to see Bay Adair again.

Why her? Why now? Why did she affect him in a way no other woman had managed to? She made him feel like he did when he jumped out of a plane or skimmed down the face of a massive wave. He loved adrenaline, adored the thrill, the kick of his heartbeat, the dry taste of fear in his mouth, feeling alive, powerful, like the world made sense.

He had experienced all that when he kissed Bay Adair earlier today.

Madness. But it was a madness he couldn't resist.

Digby pushed his hand through his hair. He never pretended to be a monk; he was a virile, healthy single guy in the prime of his life and he enjoyed women, liked sex and refused to apologize for that. He never gave anyone false hope or empty promises, treated his partners with respect and hopefully, kindness, and managed to remain friends with most of his previous lovers. Because of his parents' hedonistic lifestyle played out in the world's tabloid press, he only dated women who were single, childless and unencumbered. He never dated women who had any type of baggage.

And Bay had baggage. And lots of it.

But, when he kissed Bay earlier, he felt like he was rushing down a black-diamond ski run or increasing the lean on his superbike to negotiate a tight hairpin curve. Up until this point, women and chasing adrenaline were two of his favorite pastimes, but when he held Bay in his arms, both gelled, morphed and became one.

And that, folks, was why he was traveling to Bo Kaap at half past eight at night, to return a stuffed toy. It was also why he had to keep a firm rein on his emotions, to control what he was thinking and how he was reacting. It was easy to confuse attraction and lust with affection, desire with connection.

He was looking for a lover, not the love of his life.

Love, after all, was easily imitated and just as easily destroyed. Through neglect, death or disappearance. Love, if it existed at all, was intensely fragile and something to be avoided at all costs.

Digby knew he'd entered the Bo Kaap neighborhood when he started to notice the brightly colored houses dotting this exceptionally pretty area. Digby remembered his history, that back in the eighteenth and early nineteenth centuries, the houses in this neighborhood were leased to the slaves the British brought in from Southeast Asia and beyond. The leased houses had to be painted white back then but when the Malays were granted their freedom and were allowed to buy their houses, some of the new owners embraced color. After apartheid ended, bright, bold and stunning color swept through the neighborhood as a way for the owners to express their joy at true freedom.

He turned right, passed a tangerine-orange house, then a lime-green house, looking for number twenty.

The house Bay lived in was bright pink; the color reminded him of cartoon flamingos. Searching for a parking space, he spied an empty spot three houses down and whipped the Maserati into it, grateful for power steering. After exiting the car, he locked the door with the keyless lock and shoved the remote into his pants pocket and strolled up the street to Bay's glossy navy blue door, lifting his hand to acknowledge the kids across the street who were already making their way over to look at his car.

His Maserati tended to attract attention...

But then again attracting attention was something the Tempest-Vane family knew how to do. Digby banged his fist on her front door, waited a minute and finally heard footsteps on the wooden floor. The door cracked open and his heart settled as his eyes connected with hers.

What was it about her that made him relax, that pushed the tension from his body? No one had ever had this effect on him before and he had to get this craziness under control.

"It's about bloody time," Bay muttered, flinging the door open. She snatched the toy from his hand. "Do you have any idea of the hell I've gone through today?"

He was right about her looking exhausted; her eyes were red rimmed—had she been crying?—and her face looked a shade paler. He smiled at her outfit: a pair of loose cotton pants and a tank top showing off her slim but still sexy body.

Before he could respond to her fiery greeting, Digby felt a small bump against his legs and looked down, astounded to see a mop of ebony curls and two tiny arms encircling his leg. He found his balance and heard deep, snotty sobs coming from the little girl.

Aw, crap. The little girl tipped her head back and his breath caught at huge round wet eyes the color of obsidian. She lifted her arms up and Digby, who tended to avoid children as much and as often as possible, immediately scooped her up and placed her on his hip. She took the sloth Bay held out to her and her sobs immediately stopped. She tucked the toy into her tiny chest and rested her head on his shoulder, her thumb in her mouth.

"I finded Fluffy."

Bay nodded and held out her hands, obviously expecting the little girl to fall into her arms. Olivia surprised them all by shaking her head and laying it back on his shoulder. "Tired, Mommy Bay, and my head hurts."

"I'm sure you are, baby girl," Bay crooned, her hands still outstretched, "so let's get you into bed."

"Nuh-uh. Stay here with Fluffy's friend."

Now, there was a name he'd never been called before.

Digby patted Olivia on her tiny back. "Sweetheart, I need you to go back to your mama," he told the sweet-smelling handful in his arms.

Olivia immediately let out a screech and wrapped her arms around his neck, squeezing with everything she had. "No! Stay here."

Bay pulled a face. "Sorry. She's just feeling sick and has a bad cold," she explained.

Digby winced, thinking of his designer suit. Yay, snot and tears, just what he needed. Thank God he was as healthy as a horse and never got sick. Not knowing what else to do, he kept patting her back, keeping his touch light. A minute or so later, he heard her sigh, felt a tiny puff of breath against his neck and her tiny body sag. He lifted his eyebrows at Bay, who had a satisfied look on her face.

"She's asleep," she mouthed, gesturing for him to follow her.

Digby walked into a tiny second bedroom, white and pink, and laid the little girl into a single bed. She tried to open her eyes but when he tucked the sloth into the crook of her arm, she rolled over, yanked her legs up and fell deeper into sleep.

Bay pulled up a light blanket, kissed her head and then they both left the room. In the passage, Bay closed her eyes and her lips moved in what Digby thought might be a heartfelt prayer.

"I need a drink." Bay softly muttered, leading him into the small living room.

The room was a pale, creamy pink and the fronds of a huge fern tumbled off a side table. Seascapes adorned the wall, along with a huge photograph of a dark-skinned man holding a gorgeous strawberry blonde in his arms. Digby immediately saw the resemblance between the woman and Bay; she had to be her sister. And Olivia had inherited her father's black hair and wide, smiling mouth. They'd been a good-looking couple, Digby thought, and looked so vibrant and happy.

Like Jack, they'd died young, before they could even start to tap into their potential. Digby squared his shoulders, trying to push that familiar pain away.

Then Digby looked at Bay and he felt lighter and brighter. The pain was still there but it felt toothless and weak. How did she manage to do that?

"Let's go onto the veranda—that way we won't disturb Liv. She normally sleeps like the dead but let's not take the chance."

He'd kill for a solid eight hours. He hadn't slept for more than a few hours a night, four at the most, since Jack died. And lately, when he did sleep, he dreamed of burying Radd.

Not exactly restful.

Hoping that Bay didn't notice his shudder, Digby walked through the small sitting room and open French doors onto a tiny patio with a garden the size of a postage stamp. Herbs—he recognized lavender and parsley and mint—spilled from pots and tinged the air with their fragrant scents.

Bay gestured to a small wrought iron table, covered with colored pencils and a sketch-book. A half-full glass of white wine glistened with condensation and Digby wondered whether she'd offer him a glass.

Bay sent him a small smile and told him to take a seat. "I've had an exceptionally crappy day—I'm sorry if I was rude or snappy. Thank you for delivering Liv's favorite toy." The next words out of her mouth were the ones he really needed to hear. "Can I offer you a drink?"

He nodded and sat down, stretching out his legs and crossing his feet at the ankles.

"Whiskey or wine?"

"Whiskey would be great, thank you."

Bay nodded and turned to walk back into the house, narrow hips swinging. She had a truly exceptional ass; Digby couldn't help noticing.

Needing something to distract him from the party in his pants, Digby looked down at the table, his eyes taking in the upside-down sketch. Recognition flared and he sat up slowly, before twisting the pad. It was a rough sketch of the ballroom at The Vane, *his* ballroom.

Instead of plain white paint, the walls were covered in a subtle pattern—wallpaper?—and huge, luscious plants sat on simple, stylish pedestals. The curtain treatment was luxurious and sophisticated but not ostentatious...

Digby hauled in a quick breath.

This, *this* was what he wanted. Somehow, with barely any input from him at all, she'd nailed the brief.

Forgetting that it was her sketchbook, that he had no right to invade her privacy, he grabbed the pad and started flipping pages. She'd started a sketch for the honeymoon suite, another room he wanted redecorated, but it was only a preliminary sketch and didn't give him an idea of what she was thinking. Her next sketch was of Olivia, easily capturing the mischief in her eyes and the perfect curve of her chubby cheek. Bay was a talented artist, he thought, flipping back to the sketch of the ballroom.

Man, she'd completely captured the look he was going for.

Digby heard her approach and didn't try to hide the fact that he'd been snooping. "Your sketches are amazing."

Bay's eyes jumped from the pad to his face and back again. She handed him his whiskey before sitting down opposite him and crossing one long leg over the other. "It's how I relax," Bay replied, before taking a hefty sip of her wine. "I needed a distraction this afternoon so I started to sketch."

He was scared to say it, in case he was making a mistake—she was an inexperienced designer without a track record—but what other option did he have? He wanted the hotel revamped and Bay was the first person who'd come even close to giving him what he wanted.

"I love it—it's bloody fantastic." He pointed to the sketch and tapped the paper with his index finger. "That is exactly what I want."

Almost as much as he wanted her.

Bay's eyes widened, obviously surprised by his emphatic statement. "It is?"

Digby nodded. "Yeah." Very much so. On *both* accounts.

Excitement flashed across her face and her eyes turned a lighter shade of gold. Then the excitement faded, she bit her lip and looked away. "Thank you, I guess."

Digby frowned, wondering why she looked like he'd popped her favorite balloon. "I'm trying to offer you a job, Bay."

"I realize that."

She'd succeeded where many of the best designers in the world had failed. Why was she acting like he'd offered her a lump of coal on Christmas morning?

Digby watched as Bay played with the fabric of her cotton pants, carefully folding it into pleats on her thigh. Her hair fell down the sides of her face and he saw that she was biting the inside of her lip, her thoughts a hundred miles away.

"You do want this job, don't you? I mean, that's why you met with me today."

Bay stood up and stepped onto the tiny-sized lawn, digging her bare toes into the rich verdant grass. She held her wineglass against her chest, her eyes troubled. "Of course I would like the job but—"

Digby folded his arms and waited for her to verbalize her thoughts.

She pushed the fingertips of her hand into

her forehead and wrinkled her nose. "I have to be honest, Mr. Tempest-Vane."

"We kissed so I'm pretty sure you can call me Digby."

Bay blushed and he worked hard to hide his smile. He couldn't remember when last he'd seen a woman blush, and he rather liked the fact that she did.

Bay ignored his comment and drew patterns on the grass with her big toe. "I pretty much knew, before I even arrived at The Vane, that I wasn't experienced, or established, enough to handle the project. I shouldn't have wasted your time..."

But she had. And he was curious to know why. And, because they'd shared that intense kiss, pretty damn grateful she had.

Instead of explaining why she felt it okay to carry on with their meeting instead of canceling it, Bay veered off. "Look, I can do the design—I think I know what you are looking for, but I'm not set up to take on a big project, financially or otherwise. To be honest, while I have a diploma in interior design, I've only done a couple of small projects—"

"How small?" Digby asked, interrupting her.

She pulled a face. "A couple of kids' bedrooms and a sitting room or two."

Crap. That wasn't inexperienced, that was home decor.

"And when I say that I decorated the rooms, I accompanied my friends to the shops and advised them what to buy. Then I painted their walls and rearranged their furniture," Bay admitted.

Wonderful.

"I've applied for jobs in the sector but nobody is hiring, and you were my last, and only, chance at working in a field I love. But I knew I was very out of my depth."

Bay walked back over to the table, sat down and started to put her pencils back in their cardboard box, and in the correct order. Greens, then blues, then the red shades...who did that?

Digby reluctantly added curiosity about her to his unwanted fascination.

She was different, unusual and captivating.

Strange because those weren't emotions he was familiar with. Digby seldom delved beneath the surface with people. He liked them well enough—and the world saw him as an extrovert, someone always up for a good time—but he didn't open up, or let people in. The term *extroverted introvert* fitted him perfectly.

He could be the life of the party one night, and he could also be the guy slinking away as soon as he could the next night. And he never, ever allowed anyone to look beneath his charming exterior. Who wanted to see chaos, anyway?

Bay placed her forearms on the table and tapped her fingers against the smooth skin of her bare arm. "The long and short of it is that I'm simply not in the position to work for you."

She was right. Digby lifted his glass to his lips, allowing the whiskey to slide down his throat. He couldn't afford to have someone inexperienced running the project; the renovations had to happen quickly, causing minimal disruption to the guests. That meant teams of laborers working in shifts, coordination of deliveries, sourcing furniture and supplies.

He needed someone with experience in

these types of projects, someone who knew how to crack the whip, who could negotiate with suppliers and who had excellent time-management skills.

Bay wasn't that person. She could be, in the future, but she wasn't experienced enough to handle a project of this magnitude. But she was completely suited to be his designer because she was the only one who'd managed to capture what he wanted, design-wise. That, up until now, had proved impossible.

Digby, a million thoughts flying around his head, stood up and, echoing Bay's actions, paced the small area behind the table, his hands in his pockets, picking his problem apart.

"If I gave you the job, what would be your first step?"

Bay rolled her eyes in exasperation but eventually answered him. "I'd set up mood boards for each room, do detailed sketches, source pictures of the furniture I think would work. I'd give you a detailed drawing of my vision which we can discuss." She wrinkled her pretty nose. "I'm pretty anal when it comes to decor—everything has to be perfect. Lines have to be straight, upholstery has to be perfect, patterns have to match perfectly."

Exactly what he needed for The Vane.

Bay was what he needed, and what *she* needed was a project manager. Something he could do in his sleep…

Digby shook his head, lost in his thoughts. He couldn't possibly be thinking he'd project manage the renovation of The Vane? He had the holding company to run, the hotel to oversee. There were a dozen other projects that should take precedence until he found someone to take over the renovation of the hotel in its entirety. And it had been weeks since he'd had any spare time; if he wanted to compete in the grueling Roof of Africa motorcycle rally next year, he should do some training. And it had been an age since he surfed or skydived or even took a weekend off.

If he took on the role of project manager, working with Bay, he might be able to find some spare time in, maybe, five years or so.

But renovating The Vane was close to his heart, it always had been. Many of the good memories he had of his childhood took place within its high stone walls. He recalled playing tennis with his brothers, Jack teaching him to swim in the smaller of the three pools. His grandfather's sixtieth birthday party, Jack's twenty-first. Trying to keep up with his brothers as they scoffed down the delicious treats on offer during high tea.

So many memories…

Because he had an emotional connection to the place, there was no way he would leave any interior designer to his or her own devices. He was a control freak and he knew he'd spend a lot of time looking over shoulders, checking on the progress, making sure they were on track and keeping the standards high. If he took on the project management and Bay provided the design ideas, he'd be in control of the renovation.

And that was a situation he was fully comfortable with. And let's be honest, it would probably be a hell of a lot cheaper than hiring the best designers in the world. Not that money was an issue but Digby didn't believe in wasting cash when he didn't need to.

"Together, we could do this together," Digby

murmured, feeling the flicker of excitement in his belly growing into a fire.

"What are you talking about?" Bay demanded, placing her heels on the edge of her chair and wrapping her arms around her knees.

Digby pushed his hand through his hair and gripped the back of a wrought iron chair. "Work for me. Be my designer. I'll be the project manager, will provide the cash and funding and source the crew."

He watched her eyes widen, excitement flashing then fading. "I'd love to but, jeez, Digby, I don't think I can."

"Why on earth not?" Digby demanded, unable to believe she was passing up this opportunity. "If you work with me, you will not only be earning an excellent salary. You can say that you were the designer on a hell of a project. Provided you do a good job, and I don't see why you wouldn't, I would be happy to write a letter of recommendation for you. Working for me would open up a lot of doors for you."

"I understand that and I'm grateful for the

offer but it's not that simple!" Bay cried, standing up abruptly. "Can I be honest?"

"Please do."

"I didn't really think this through. I was so caught up in the design work and forgot about the practicalities of working for you, working for anyone, actually. I'm guessing that there would be very tight time constraints, wouldn't there?"

"Yeah, obviously. Shutting anything down means losing money so, yes, you'd have to work long hours and plenty of overtime. You'd be recompensed accordingly."

Bay twisted her lips. "But that's my problem, Digby. I can't work long hours and loads of overtime. I'm responsible for a little girl who lost both her parents six months ago and who is, I'm quite sure, suffering from separation anxiety. While I desperately need an income, and a steady job, I can't leave her for extended periods. I especially can't leave her alone at night and Mama B is too old to look after a three-year-old every day."

Digby stared at her and scratched his head. Damn, he'd forgotten about Olivia. And he remembered how he felt, as a young teenager losing Jack—he'd suffered terribly and had clung to Radd—so he understood Olivia's fear of losing Bay.

Hell, he was *still* terrified that he was going to lose Radd. As his dreams kept reminding him.

But he couldn't lose Bay's talents either. If he did, he didn't know how long it would take before he found someone else who got him.

Got his vision, got what he wanted for The Vane, he clarified.

He thought for a minute, then a minute more. "What if you brought Olivia to work with you?" he asked.

"Then I would get no work done," Bay crisply replied. "She's sweet and lovely but she's demanding. And willful.

"And she doesn't trust strangers," Bay added.

"She seemed to trust me," Digby said.

"I know and that was super strange. But you did bring Fluffy back so... Are you offering to look after her while I work?" Bay asked him. She smiled. "I give you a half a day and you'll be begging me for mercy."

"She can't be that bad," Digby protested.

"She's worse," Bay cheerfully replied. She hesitated, started to speak and shook her head.

Digby encouraged her to voice her thoughts and after a moment she spoke again. "Maybe I can do the drawings for you, set up the mood boards for you, and you can take it from there. You can pay me for doing that."

Digby thought about her suggestion and pretty much instantly dismissed it. "I worked on the design of Kagiso Lodge with Radd, and things we thought would work on paper sometimes didn't. I'd need you to be there to give immediate input, to make changes on the fly."

"That's fair." Bay's expression closed down and she lifted her shoulders in a weary shrug. "I appreciate your offer, Digby, and your faith in my work, but I just don't see how it would work. And I don't want to start something, be excited about it and have it come crashing down around my ears. I desperately need a stable, secure job."

He heard the tension in her voice, saw the way her fists clenched and opened and thought that there was a lot Bay wasn't telling him. And that was okay...

For now.

"I'm prepared to offer you a decent contract," Digby informed her. "And I have an idea about what to do with Olivia..."

Bay lifted her sexy eyebrows—he'd never thought a pair of brows could be sexy until today—and waited for him to continue.

"Today I signed off on some new hires from Human Resources, including a three-month contract for an American looking for temporary work as a waitress..."

He hesitated, wondering if Bay would go for his proposal. There was only one way to find out...

CHAPTER FOUR

As DIGBY BEGAN outlining his proposal, Bay felt like she was on a Tilt-A-Whirl, or that she was a dandelion trying to survive a hurricane. What was *happening*?

Earlier this evening, she'd bathed Olivia and read her endless stories trying—and failing—to distract her from the loss of Mr. Fluffy. Finally, at the end of her rope, she'd allowed Liv to watch her favorite TV show. Leaving her to it, Bay, staying in hearing distance, had gone outside to think, knowing that she needed to make some tough decisions. Bringing her sketch pad—because thinking was so much easier when her hands were busy—she'd contemplated her options, idly drawing the ballroom at The Vane as she considered her next move.

But her thoughts had kept veering to Digby's lips on hers, remembering the feel of his strong biceps under her hands and the silky texture of his wavy hair. Remembering how sexy it had been feeling his stubble on her skin as he kissed her jaw was far more fun than contemplating her return to the world of engineering.

She'd spent five years at the university studying a subject she hated just because her father told her she shouldn't, that she'd never succeed, that it was a man's job...

Stupid.

Pulling her thoughts back to what was important, she'd tried to reach Busi again, relieved to hear her old friend's voice. But Busi hadn't any good news for her—the partners had recently resolved to place a freeze on new hires. There weren't many openings in the sector either, Busi had told her and, because she had little experience, she might find it difficult to find a position.

Awesome.

Having had enough of reality and unable to deal with any more bad news, Bay had allowed her thoughts to drift back to Digby again, recalling how good he smelled, of expensive products containing spice and lemon and something that made her brain shut down and her ovaries sit up.

Nobody had ever made her feel as out of control as Digby Tempest-Vane did.

And he should be the last guy in the world she should be attracted to. He was a player, flitting from model to actress to celebrity to princess with astounding regularity. He had a reputation, deserved or not, of being a playboy, irresponsible or, as her grandmother used to say, a flibbertigibbet. Flighty, flirty and yeah, charming.

She didn't trust charming.

But that hadn't stopped her traitorous body from wanting to plaster itself against his broad chest, to bury her nose in his strong neck, to explore the ridges of his ribbed stomach or the strength of his thighs.

Oh, Lord, she was in so much trouble.

And she knew this because, right now, although she should be thinking of his outrageous and frankly amazing proposal, she was also thinking of how he would look naked. Pretty wonderful, she imagined.

Argh! Really?

Right, time to act like an adult, Adair. Think!

He was offering her a hell of an opportunity, a way to establish a career doing what she loved, but how could she take that up without neglecting Liv? The little girl was wary of strangers and she hadn't been lying earlier—she hated being separated from Bay.

Working long hours for Digby, or anyone else, would be impossible. She needed to spend time with Liv—that was nonnegotiable. Her mental well-being was all that was important.

Along with feeding and clothing her and educating her and...

Rock, let me introduce you to Hard Place.

Bay pushed her hand through her hair, feeling like a hundred years old. Sometimes the responsibility seemed overwhelming.

Today I signed off on new hires from Human Resources, including a three-month contract for an American looking for temporary work as a waitress...

Digby's mind was, obviously, operating at warp speed. He rarely, she supposed, heard no, and she guessed that finding solutions to problems had to be something billionaires excelled at. If they didn't, they wouldn't be so rich, right?

She tightened her grip on her knees and waited for him to continue, interested in what he had to say but knowing that, eventually, he'd walk out of her house and her life.

That was just the way life worked. He was a rich, free-as-a-bird playboy; she was a broke, single mom trying to survive.

"The waitress I hired has a degree in early childhood education and has experience working in her mom's playschool in San Francisco. What if I hired her to look after Olivia?"

Bay blinked, not sure if she'd heard him correctly. "What?"

"We have specialized programs at The Vane to entertain children so that their parents can eat in our Michelin-starred restaurant, drink cocktails on the veranda with other adults or take quality time on their own. We do have family-friendly areas, obviously, but we aim to keep the kids entertained and I employ specialized staff to do that.

"I have a team of au pairs at the hotel but let me employ the American to look after

Olivia, exclusively. She can join the play-group if she wishes to. I don't know anything about three-year-olds, but don't they need the company of their own kind?"

Bay's lips twitched at his choice of words. But he wasn't wrong, it would be good for Liv to play with kids her own age.

"If you need to see her or spend time with her, it's a ten-minute walk across the grounds to the buildings, ditto if she needs to see you. You could work, knowing she's safe and cared for and in easy reach."

Oh, my, he'd cut away her biggest objection to working with him. He was making it exceedingly difficult to say no. And why should she? This job was the answer to her many, many prayers.

"You design, you source paint and materials and stuff you need and you request quotes. I'll organize the work crews, haggle with the suppliers for better prices and arrange for delivery."

He mentioned a monthly salary that had her eyes bugging out. Her tongue, she was sure, was an inch from the floor. She wasn't certain what the going rate for interior designers was but, man, that figure sounded like four or five times what she'd hoped to earn.

"Are you being serious?"

His deep blue eyes connected and held hers. "Deathly."

Well, then.

Bay ran her hands over her face, her mind racing with possibilities. Needing to see it on paper, she pulled her sketch pad toward her, grabbed a bright purple pencil and did a quick calculation, working out her salary for the next six months. Another quick sum gave her the figure of her expenses over the same period and there was a healthy profit. And she wouldn't have to pay for Olivia's childcare so that would increase her disposable income.

She could pay off some debts, buy Olivia a new summer wardrobe and service her car. She could also stash some money away every month for emergencies and best of all, she could afford a good lawyer to help her in her quest to keep custody of Liv.

She couldn't say no; this opportunity was heaven-sent.

Except for one thing...

"What about…" Bay hesitated, her eyes going to his sexy mouth. She bit her lip, knowing she was blushing. "…what happened earlier?"

"Do you want me to tell you that it won't happen again?" Digby asked her and she noticed that his hands were gripping the back of the chair, his knuckles white.

No. Yes. She didn't know.

"I am attracted to you, you know that," Digby said, his voice harsh but his eyes not leaving her face. "All I can promise you is that, no matter what, your job will never be in jeopardy because of anything that happens between us."

She should demand more, to make him promise that nothing would happen between them at all. *Ever.* But she couldn't make herself voice that thought.

Digby's deep blue eyes slammed into hers. "I never play where I work, Bay, and if something happened between us it would be the exception rather than the rule. What if I put the power into your hands?"

Sorry? What was he talking about? Bay frowned at him. "I don't understand."

"If you want something to happen between us, *you* make the move." His sexy mouth quirked in a half smile. "I'm not saying that I won't try to tempt you into bed, but if we get there, it'll be your choice, your timing. Your terms."

Bay's mouth fell open; she was not sure how to react. No man, not her father, either of her two previous lovers or any of her boyfriends, allowed her to be in the driving seat, to take control. Bay turned over his offer, looking for the catch. Because there had to be one. Nobody made that sort of proposal without getting something out of the arrangement.

What was Digby's angle?

She didn't trust him; she didn't trust anybody, so she shook her head. "Nothing will happen between us, Digby."

He frowned at that. "Are you involved with someone?"

She shook her head.

"No. But I can't, for a lot of reasons, get involved with you." Bay said, dropping her feet to the floor.

"It would be an affair, Bay, not an involvement," Digby told her, his voice soft, but she heard the determination in his words. So, like her, Digby wasn't looking for love or commitment. She wondered if his reasons were as complicated as hers.

It didn't matter; they weren't going to go there. Her life was convoluted enough without adding an affair with her employer to the list of things guaranteed to stress her out.

She saw his flash of disappointment when she didn't offer a reason, but she couldn't, wouldn't explain. She was a private person, used to keeping her own counsel. She'd spent too many years fighting with her father for her voice to be heard, her opinions respected, only to be dismissed and rejected, so she'd decided, a long time ago, to keep her thoughts to herself. If she didn't share them, they couldn't be stomped on.

Bay thrust the purple pencil in his direction. Digby raised his thick eyebrows and took the pencil. "And what do you want me to do with this?"

"Scribble a note about providing a nanny for Liv and sign your name next to my calculations and we'll take that as a preliminary contract. You can send me an official one later."

Digby nodded and bent over her sketch pad, his hand dashing words across her page. His signature, bold and confident, just like the man, followed. He straightened, placed the pencil in the box and sent her a small smile. He held out his hand for her to shake. "Deal?"

Bay had no choice but to place her hand in his, trying to ignore the tingles racing up her arm and the heat settling in her belly. "Deal. When do you want me to start?"

He nodded to her sketch pad. "You already have, Bay. Keep doing that and I'll be in touch in a day or two."

Digby released her hand and walked around the table, dropping his head so that his lips were close to hers, sending anticipation and heat swirling through her. "I thought you said that I was in the driving seat."

Digby had the temerity to grin at her. "And you are. But I told you I'd try and tempt you, remember?" He stood so close to her that all she'd have to do was tilt her head upwards and… "Are you tempted, Bay?" Digby whispered the words against her lips.

Desperately so. But Bay didn't think that the superconfident Digby needed to hear that. He was far too cocky as it was…

"Good. Night, Bay."

Bay watched, openmouthed as he walked into her house and out of sight. Then she heard the front door closing behind him and dropped her forehead to the table, feeling both exhilarated and unbalanced, thanks to Digby's professional offer and the heat in his eyes.

And Bay knew that the contradictory feelings wouldn't disappear anytime soon.

Digby sat on the edge of his desk and watched Bay introduce Olivia to her new nanny, Roisin. Row-sheen, he remembered, was the way her name was pronounced. It was Irish, the tall, dark-haired American had explained. And, yes, she was happy to look after Olivia…

Excellent news.

When Roisin tipped her head to the side to explain something to Olivia, she looked a little familiar but Digby immediately dismissed the thought. Roisin had a strong American accent and she'd only been in the country for a month, having flown out from San Francisco six weeks ago, so he couldn't have met her before.

His thoughts moved on from Roisin to Bay, looking fresh and lovely in a pale pink sleeveless shirt and tan capri pants, funky sneakers on her small feet. She wasn't conventionally pretty but something about her kept her constantly on his mind.

In between imagining what she looked like naked, he also had random questions about her, like was she a coffee-first-thing-in-the-morning type of person and did she prefer cats or dogs? Did she prefer chocolate or vanilla and how did she feel about being responsible for raising someone else's child?

In between making mental lists and planning strategies, or finding solutions to a dozen big and small problems, his thoughts often drifted to the kiss they'd shared, remembering how wonderful her mouth felt under his, how her slim body seemed to fit his perfectly, her lovely, subtle scent and the spice of her mouth. And how the world seemed to stop spinning whenever she was in the room, how his heart settled and sighed whenever she was around.

God, he had to stop thinking like this. This wasn't who he was, what he did.

She was taking up far too much of his mental energy. He couldn't offer her anything; he wasn't capable of long-term relationships or even wanted one. Oh, he could play the part of the charming rogue, the life and soul of any party, but he was, deep down where honesty resided, a loner, someone completely comfortable with living his life solo. He'd had parents who never paid him any attention growing up—hell, he remembered not seeing them once over six months—and when they were around, they ignored him to focus on their pursuit of pleasure.

But he and his parents did share some common traits. Like them, he liked his freedom, liked being able to do what he wanted when he wanted, without having to answer to a wife or significant other. But the difference between him and his parents was that he realized how hurtful neglect and disinterest could be and he'd never ever do that to a partner or a child.

Besides, he'd never risk loving and losing someone again. Radd had been, for the past twenty years, his only anchor, all the family he wanted, needed or could cope with.

So why was he, mentally, linking Bay with thoughts of his family? God only knew. What he was certain of was that seeing her, working with her and knowing she was solidly off-limits was going to make the next few months pure torture.

Fingers snapping in front of his face pulled him back to the present. He blinked and Bay's amused face came back into focus. "There you are. Did you take a nice trip?"

Digby looked around his office to find it empty. "Where did they go?"

"To the nursery. Liv was more than happy to go with her, thank God," Bay told him, her eyes reflecting her relief. Her eyes turned to gold when she was happy, darkened when she was stressed. *Good to know*, Digby thought.

Bay placed her hand on his biceps and squeezed and Digby realized it was the first time she'd initiated physical contact. The heat of her hand burned through his cotton to brand him.

"Thank you for hiring Roisin—she's amazing."

Digby risked placing his hand on her hip and moving her so that she stood between his outstretched legs. "Pleasure," he murmured, his hand skating over her hip bone.

Digby looked down into her face and saw the blue stripes under her eyes. Wondering why he hadn't noticed how tired she was, he pulled back, just a little, to look at her properly. Her shoulders were hunched and the cords in her neck were pulled tight.

She was stressed to the max.

She had a job and a nanny for Olivia, so what else was worrying her? And why was he so desperate to know, and worse, to fix, all her problems, to protect her from anything that was causing her pain?

Lifting his hand, he clasped the back of her neck and rested his forehead on hers. "Are you okay, Bay? Can I do anything, anything at all, to help you?"

Bay's extraordinary eyes met his and he saw a brief hint of tears. She opened her mouth to speak but then snapped it closed before shaking her head.

Instead of answering his questions, she rested her head on his collarbone and placed her hands on his waist. Her next words weren't something he expected. "Can you, for just a minute, hold me, Dig?"

Dig.

Nobody else but Radd and Muzi shortened his name and he liked hearing it on her lips. And, while hugs weren't something people, specifically women, associated with him, he was more than happy to wrap his arms around her and pull her in close.

And, he acknowledged, this had nothing to do with sex and attraction; she was looking for, needed, something else from him. Comfort, maybe? Support? Did it matter? Maybe not.

"Come here, kid."

Digby didn't give her a chance to object, or rethink her question, he just wrapped her up, holding her tight. He placed his cheek on her hair and smiled when her arms encircled his waist to hug him back. They were in his office and they had a ton of work to do but he'd hold her for as long as she needed.

Anytime. Anywhere.

And strangely enough, at that moment, with her in his arms, the thought didn't scare him as much as it should.

"Mama B, Roisin is wonderful. Liv has really taken to her," Bay explained, her phone tucked between her neck and shoulder.

"I want to meet her, to decide for myself," Mama B replied, her tone suggesting that Bay not argue.

Bay grinned, knowing that Mama B's concern came from a place of great love. "I'll ask whether she can bring Liv to you for a play-date and you can meet her then. You'll like her. I promise."

"We'll see," Mama B replied, before abruptly ending the call. Bay grinned. Mama B had said what she said and was done talking. Bay envied the freedom that came with being old.

Bay, sitting cross-legged on Digby's sofa, put her pencil down and stretched, raising her arms high above her head and bending from side to side. When she was traveling, she'd carved out time to do daily yoga and Pilates sessions, but since returning to Cape Town, yoga and any form of exercise had fallen by the wayside.

God, she missed it. She also missed quiet cups of coffee in the morning, the excitement of buying a ticket to a new destination and stepping off the plane to soak in the sights and sounds of a different land and culture. The noisiness of Bangkok, the sophistication of Florence, the serenity of Bhutan.

She missed the feeling of only being responsible for herself, being able to act with spontaneity and being as free as one could be in the twenty-first century.

As always, a wave of guilt broke over her and she felt terrible for mourning her free, uncomplicated and easy life. *And let's remember why you aren't in Kathmandu or Kampala right now, Adair, and that's because your sister is* dead.

If she handed over custody of Liv to her parents, like they wanted her to do, then she could return to traveling, to exploring the world. She could go to Iran, or to Alaska, or she could pick up a job working on the yachts in the Med.

But how could she enjoy, well, anything, knowing that Layla's little girl would be at the mercy of her rigid, controlling and austere parents?

Initially, Bay knew, her parents would shower her with love and affection, and Liv would be the happiest little girl alive. She'd blossom and shine but, if she was anything like her mom and aunt, as she hit her teens she'd start to question the rules, the rigidity, the lack of trust and their protectiveness. She'd want to spread her wings and they'd be clipped. There would be lectures and then more lectures, and if those didn't work, attention would be withdrawn and love withheld. Affection would become a thing of the past. And because she was strong-willed and stubborn, Olivia wouldn't back down but would be left swinging in the wind, unsure and alone and feeling like she was dying inside.

Bay knew exactly what that felt like.

She thought back to her meeting the previous day with her new lawyer, a friend of Busi's, and to the million questions she'd answered about her life, her job and her romantic interests. Gillian Crawford had deep dived into her life and Bay had told her about her altercation with her father and admitted to her attraction to Digby.

Gillian, an experienced family lawyer, then took her through the legal process and pointed out possible pitfalls. Her parents were well respected, good people, who could give Olivia every opportunity. Because they had children young, they were only in their early fifties and they were fit and could keep up with a three-year-old.

They were perfect.

Bay, on the other hand, was not. She was single, and while her new job working for Digby was a good start, it wasn't permanent and, thanks to her traveling, it could be argued that her lifestyle was a trifle unstable.

But, Gill continued, Layla and Ali wanted her to have custody of Olivia, not her parents. The judge would, probably, respect their wishes.

Unless she gave the judge cause to question her judgment.

Until this lawsuit went away, her lawyer

also advised her to downplay her connection to Digby Tempest-Vane. Working for him was one thing, but if the press linked them together romantically, they could and would make a meal of her supposed relationship with the playboy billionaire. Digby was a guy who played hard and fast, who hadn't had a long-term relationship in his life and who had been raised by the most notorious and dissolute couple on the continent.

Her name linked with his would result in her judgment being questioned and that was something that needed to be, at all costs, avoided.

Damn, it wasn't right. Sure, Digby's parents had indulged in drugs and affairs and wild parties—orgies had been mentioned on numerous occasions—but they'd died two years ago and she didn't think it fair for Digby to be judged by the sins of his parents.

It was so unfair that the only man she'd been attracted to in ages was the one man she had to avoid. But, fair or not, she couldn't risk losing Liv.

Nor would she risk allowing herself to bask in his affection and attention. He'd jerk both away when he was done with her, when she no longer interested him, and she'd be left feeling hollow and empty again.

But, like a child who'd been told not to eat the sweets she'd been left alone with, all she wanted to do was gorge herself on him. To taste his wonderful mouth again, to push his shirt up his chest to reveal his exceptional body, to scrape her teeth along his jaw, tug his earlobe in her mouth, put her hands down his—

Whoa, boy! Getting a bit hot in here. Putting her sketch pad aside, Bay stood up, walked over to the window and stared past the incredible rose garden to Table Mountain, covered with its rolling tablecloth. *You can't think about Digby like that, Bay, it's too dangerous.*

She knew it but it was so damn hard, especially when the man was temptation on two feet.

Bay heard his footsteps behind her and felt his hands on her shoulders. She knew she should step away, but when his hands skated down her arms, to slide across her stomach, she leaned back into him, enjoying the way his arms encircled her waist. It was so nice to have human contact, to have a hard man with big arms holding her tight. To feel like she wasn't quite so alone...

"Tempting me again, Tempest-Vane?"

"Trying to," Digby replied.

Bay felt Digby's lips on her neck, sighed when his teeth scraped over the sensitive cord of her throat, along her jaw. She had to stop this, and she would, in a minute. Bay wanted just one minute to enjoy his scent and his solidity, his masculinity and the way he electrified every inch of her body.

"Is it working?" Digby quietly asked.

Bay turned to face him, resting her hands on his chest. "You know it is and it's so unfair."

"You should know that I don't play fair, sweetheart." Digby pulled her in close, her breasts pushing into his pale blue button-down shirt. Her nipples hardened and Digby placed his hand on her back, a fraction above her butt, pulled her hips to him, and Bay sighed at the hard ridge in his pants.

Yeah, she really should step away...

But he did tempt her and, damn, she wanted

just one quick kiss. One *last* kiss. Bay, silently, cursed herself and her lack of control. She had to pull herself together; she couldn't afford to allow him to wear her down, to put herself in a situation that would have huge consequences for Olivia. She couldn't give in to the madness he pulled to the surface; there was too much at stake. She wasn't the only one who had skin in the game and she had to make the best possible choices to keep her tiny family together.

Transient pleasure, a few hours in Digby's arms, wasn't worth the risk.

Digby was far too good at this temptation game, Bay conceded. She'd step away soon, she *would*, she just needed a minute.

That minute passed, and Bay didn't move away, she simply *couldn't*. She wanted this, she wanted him.

"Time is up, sweetheart."

Digby's lips covered hers but Bay, despite her frustration at being so damn weak, didn't hesitate. She immediately invited him in. His tongue, wet and wild, slid across hers and Bay whimpered, loving his heat and his intensity. He wanted her, of that she had no doubt. She felt his desire in the way his gentle fingers traced the line of her jaw, roamed over her lower back before he was digging his fingertips into her butt and groaning into her mouth.

She could stand here in the morning sun and kiss him endlessly, drinking in his power and earthiness, spice and strength. He was *such* a man, strong and hard and rough and sexy. Everything she'd never known she needed in a lover.

He wouldn't treat her like a fragile flower; he'd demand that she give him everything she could, and then he'd teach her to give up more. Bay had no doubt he could persuade her to give him everything...

But that wasn't possible. She needed to keep their relationship professional and Digby at a distance. Right now, they couldn't slide a piece of paper between them.

Bay wrenched her mouth off his and slapped her hands against his chest, pushing against his strength. Digby resisted, just for a second or two, and then he stepped back, lifting his hands off her to scrub his face.

"Dammit."

Bay didn't know whether he was upset with her or himself, but it didn't matter, this couldn't happen again. She had to resist him; she was playing with fire. If the circumstances were different, there was a chance she'd say to hell with it and sleep with the gorgeous man. It would be highly unusual, but there was a first time for everything.

But, if anyone linked them together, Liv's custody battle could be affected by her actions and that was intolerable. She would not risk her future, or her heart, for a quick, or slow, orgasm.

She was bigger and better than that.

She hoped.

CHAPTER FIVE

BAY HAD BARELY managed to pull Olivia's pajama shorts up her chubby legs before the little girl took off down the short hallway, running as fast as she could to get back to Digby.

Her little girl had a crush, Bay thought. Her new mama did too.

He'd been caught up at Tempest-Vane HQ today and they hadn't had time to discuss her suggested color and decor schemes for the hotel. When Digby suggested that he come to her place, she'd been hesitant. What if the press followed him here? The assumption would be that they were lovers and she couldn't, in light of her custody battle, allow that to happen.

But she hadn't had the willpower to say no. And they did need to catch up on work...

Too late now, he was here.

Bay sighed and followed Liv to where Digby

sat on the small patio, a glass of whiskey at his elbow. As she suspected, Olivia, and Fluffy, were in his lap and her sweet head rested on his broad shoulder, her thumb in her mouth and her eyes heavy.

She'd be asleep in minutes, Bay realized. Roisin had taken her swimming in The Vane's family pool this afternoon and Liv had by all accounts loved every second of being in the water and had no fear.

But, after a full day, the little girl was completely exhausted.

A glass of wine, courtesy of Digby, sat on the wrought iron table and Bay took a sip, allowing the icy and tart liquid to slide down her throat. Cape Town was experiencing a heat wave. Her cottage didn't have air-conditioning and she felt like she was about to melt.

In contrast to her, Digby looked cool and comfortable in chino shorts and a loose linen shirt, flip-flops on his sexy feet. He'd asked for some time tonight—they hadn't finished their discussion about her mood boards—and Bay invited him to her cottage any time after six. He arrived, to both her and Liv's delight, at six fifteen.

Bay sighed and rubbed the back of her neck in frustration. She wanted, much to her chagrin, to spend as much time with Digby as possible, even though he was dangerous to her self-control.

And her future…

He was *that* addictive.

But addictive or not, it was very annoying that he'd found the time to have a shower before arriving at her door and Bay frowned. She hadn't had a moment to herself after collecting Olivia from Roisin. Before making her way home, she'd needed to stop and buy some groceries, hit a cash machine and put fuel in her car. When she got home, she had to feed and bathe a fractious Olivia. And if she didn't put laundry in tonight they'd have no clothes because they were out of, well, everything.

Bay felt like she'd run a marathon. The idea of making herself something to eat was a step, or ten too far. No wonder she was dropping weight. And God, she hoped Digby didn't expect dinner.

"I'm not cooking," Bay told him, feeling defiant. Her mother, no matter how long a day she'd had, would've made sure her father had a two-course meal ready the moment he stepped through the door.

She was not her mother; she would *never* be her mother. And Digby was her boss, not her lover or boyfriend or husband.

Digby raised his eyebrows at the rather snippy tone. "I know—that's why I ordered Chinese. You do like Chinese, don't you?"

Who didn't? "Sure, I like Chinese." Feeling embarrassed, she sat down on the chair opposite him and hiked her heels up onto the seat. She rubbed her eyes with the balls of her hands. "Sorry, it's been a long day."

"For me too, and I didn't have to deal with the human dynamo," Digby replied. He looked down at Olivia, his face reflecting his confusion. "I don't understand why she likes me. I've had zero interaction with kids."

Bay smiled at his statement. "I think it's a gut thing. She immediately liked Roisin, as well. I trust those initial impressions."

Digby picked up his whiskey glass with his

spare hand. "Did you also trust Roisin immediately?"

Bay heard an uncertain note in his voice and cocked her head. "I did. Didn't you?"

Digby seemed to choose his words carefully. "About her qualifications and her love for children, I did. But there's something…"

"What?" Bay asked. She'd spent enough time with Digby to realize that under that very hot face and exceptional body was a scalpel-sharp brain. If he had concerns about Roisin then she'd listen. "Should we be looking for another nanny for Liv?"

The thought made her heart sink. Liv loved Roisin and was completely comfortable with her. Even Mama B liked her, enough to offer to teach Roisin how to make her famous bobotie, something she rarely did. Finding another nanny would not be easy.

Digby held up his hand, his expression wry. "No, relax. I have absolute faith in her ability to look after this peanut." Digby patted Liv's thigh. "I'm not sure that I believe that she's in Africa just because she's traveling…" Digby stared at his whiskey before shrugging. "But her personal life has nothing to do with me."

Bay glanced at Olivia and saw that the little girl was fast asleep on Digby's chest. She gestured to her. "I can take her and put her to bed if you like."

"You just sat down," Digby pointed out, "and she weighs about as much as a feather."

Bay sipped her wine and rolled her head on her shoulders, trying to work out some of the knots in her neck.

She looked at Digby, who was looking very at ease despite the soft bundle lying on his chest. But he did look tired and his fabulous eyes had dark rings under them. Because she was sharing his office at The Vane, she knew how many balls he had up in the air. His meetings and calls never stopped. "You're looking a bit shattered too, Digby. When are you expecting your brother back?"

Digby shrugged. "God knows. He's been away for a few weeks already and I am hoping that he'll be back in time to help cohost our View of Table Mountain Ball."

Bay had heard of the ball—it was one of the premier social events on Cape Town's social calendar. The tickets were stunningly expensive, hard to come by and were snapped up months before the event. The ball raised funds for numerous causes throughout the city, including HIV/AIDS clinics, literacy and school feeding programs.

The attendees were the most influential, richest and powerful people in the country, including politicians, kingmakers and captains of industry.

"This year is the centenary anniversary of the ball—my great-great-grandmother hosted the first ball at The Vane in 1921—so Radd, and Brin, had better bloody be there," Digby stated. "I am not dealing with that lot on my own."

Bay raised her eyebrows. "I'm sure you can host the ball on your own with one hand behind your back." He was charming and fully comfortable in every social situation, could work the crowd with ease and make everyone feel welcome and important. Radd, she'd heard, was quieter and far less sociable than his brother.

"I miss him," Digby said, surprising her with his admission. For a hugely popular guy, Digby rarely spoke about his personal life.

"Radd?" she asked, just to be clear.

"Yeah. It's been just the two of us for a long, long time and not having him around feels...strange," Digby quietly replied, his blue eyes a shade darker with an emotion she couldn't identify. Could it be loneliness? No, that didn't make sense; Digby was one of the most popular people in Cape Town and, according to everything she'd read, had a hectic social life.

"You're so lucky to have a lot of friends," Bay said. She'd been around Digby enough to realize that he was one of those rare individuals who pulled people into his orbit, someone people gravitated to.

Women wanted to be with him, men wanted to be him...

"I have a lot of acquaintances," Digby corrected her. "I only have a few people I call my friends. Radd, obviously. Muzi Miya-Matthews—"

She'd heard of Muzi Miya-Matthews; he owned and operated some of the best vineyards in the country and was the CEO of a famous wine brand. "The wine guy?"

Digby laughed. "Actually, he has a double degree in business and oenology."

Impressive. "Anyone else?" Bay asked, wanting to hear more about his private world.

Digby lifted a broad shoulder. "No, not really. I mean, I know a lot of people, but people who know me? Muzi and Radd...that's it, I guess."

Bay lowered her glass, her eyes searching his face. He wasn't being serious, she thought, because there was no way one of the most popular bachelors in the city could only call two people—two!—and one was his brother—a close friend. Hell, she'd been out of the country for years and she still had a few close friends.

Bay moved her legs, tucking her heels under her bottom. Needing to dig deeper, she tossed out another question. "Tell me what you and Radd were like as kids?"

Digby flashed his hot-as-the-sun grin. "Naughty as hell. Jack, because he was so much older than us, tried to keep us in line, and he frequently said it was like trying to herd rabid cats. Basically, we were, to a large extent, feral."

Bay smiled. She could easily imagine the

Tempest-Vane brothers causing havoc. Especially Digby. "But you grew up, eventually."

"Radd is more grown-up than me—he's even engaged. I never thought that would happen."

Digby reached for his whiskey glass and took a long swallow. He sent her a wry look and she caught the flash of embarrassment in his eyes. "I'm trying really hard to be an adult about him and Brin."

Bay cocked her head to the side. "You don't like Brin? Why not? She's lovely!"

Brin and Abby were her friends and she wouldn't listen to him, or anybody else, denigrate them.

"Relax, spitfire, I'm not about to insult her," Digby told her, his eyes amused. "I like Brin. I really do, and she's perfect for Radd."

"Then what's the problem?"

Digby stared down into his nearly empty glass, his eyes darkening to a shade off midnight. "I'm the problem, Bay. This will sound completely ridiculous since I am a guy in his midthirties but—*Jesus*."

Bay waited for him to continue, trying not to show her impatience. If she pushed, Digby would retreat and she'd never know what he was about to say.

"It's been Radd and me, against the world, since I was fourteen, fifteen years old. As you and the world know, our parents were bloody useless." Digby's already deep voice dropped an octave and she heard a slight tremor to his words. Speaking of his past wasn't easy, but she thought that it might be necessary. Everybody, even sexy playboys, needed to vent.

"Radd is, has been, the only constant in my life for two decades—" Digby's thick eyebrows pulled together and he drained his glass. "Can we talk about something else? We've both had a long day and this is depressing."

Bay shook her head. "No. Tell me what you were about to say about Radd." Yeah, she was pushing him but sometimes thoughts needed to be expressed before they festered. Though maybe that horse had already bolted...

Either way, it would be good for him to voice his frustration.

Digby glared at her, not happy to be pushed into a corner. "You're not going to let me change the subject, are you?"

Bay handed him a small smile. "Nope. Now, stop stalling and tell me."

Digby rubbed the back of his neck as his words poured out in a rush. "I'm jealous of her, jealous that she has his time and I don't. Jealous that he's not mine anymore."

Oh, Digby. Bay placed her hand on her heart but remained quiet, knowing that the dam wall had, well, not broken but cracked.

Digby's sigh was both heavy and embarrassed. "As I said, we've been on our own since our teens. Radd tended to put himself between me and the world when we were younger but, as we grew up, our relationship evened out. Our school offered a gap year after we graduated and, because there's less than a year between us, he chose to do that gap year so that we could attend the university together. We started our internet business together, developing a new payment system, worked together, planned our future together."

Digby stared at her, his expression telling her that he was ready for her to mock him, or to dismiss his fears. For someone so personable on the surface, he really wasn't good at emotionally deep conversations.

"We were a team," Digby said and Bay heard the pain in his voice.

Bay allowed her eyes to connect with his. "And now you think you're not because he's going to marry Brin?"

"Stupid, right?"

Seeing his confusion, Bay decided to put him out of his misery. "You're allowed to feel that way, Digby. Change is always scary."

"I feel like an idiot. And, worse, like a crap brother!"

"Actually, you sound human," Bay told him. "And normal."

Digby grimaced. "I sound like a moron."

Bay's lips quirked up at his low grumble and grumpy face. Unable to resist, she stood up, placed a hand on his shoulder and brushed her lips across his mouth. Funny how perceptions were often wrong, she thought. She'd genuinely believed Digby had a wide circle of friends, but what he had were acquaintances and he was, actually, emotionally isolated.

Digby lifted his free hand to hold the back of her head, to keep her mouth on his. His tongue slid into her mouth, and want and need replaced sympathy. Knowing that she was on a runaway train, Bay slammed on the brakes and lifted her mouth from his. They were venturing into emotional-connection territory, heading toward some sort of non-physical intimacy. Such connections—expressing feelings and vulnerabilities—were dangerous, especially for her. She refused to step onto that magic carpet only to crash and burn when the wind powering her flight died or changed direction.

She liked Digby, loved the way he made her body sing, but she refused to be another crash victim. Although he was becoming harder and harder to resist and here she was, giving herself more opportunities to be tempted.

Ignoring the whole custody-battle issue, there was a very real chance she could fall for Digby. And if she did that, she would get hurt. She'd throw herself at him, offer him everything, and he might, for a little time, return her affection. But then, because the man never had long-term relationships, she'd start to bore him and he'd begin looking around for something new, someone different.

Then, as her dad did, he'd pull his affection and attention and she'd be left swinging in a cold wind. God, having and losing love had hurt so damn much.

Not happening, never again.

And if that wasn't enough of a reason, she couldn't afford, according to her lawyer, to be romantically linked with Digby.

She wasn't ready to tell him, or anyone, about her custody battle. That would mean explaining that she was estranged from her parents, that they didn't think her capable of raising Liv, that her parents no longer loved her. Or even liked her.

Bay slid her hands under Liv's thighs and back and easily lifted her into her arms. "I'll put Olivia to bed and then we can get to work."

Digby frowned at her, obviously confused by her sudden change of subject. But before he could respond, the peal of her doorbell drifted through the house.

Saved, she decided, by Chinese takeout.

"Digby, you're a freaking maniac!"

A week or so later Digby laughed as he

whipped his Ducati between two minibus taxis and smiled at Bay's voice in his ear via the intercom system between their two helmets. She was tucked up behind him on his superbike, her arms around his waist, working with him as he steered his bike down the still busy Cape Town highway. Lifting one hand, he patted her slim, denim-covered thigh.

"Relax, I'm not going that fast." Okay, maybe he was going a little fast.

Digby returned his hand to the handlebar and smiled as he recalled Bay's confused face when she opened the door of her cottage earlier. She'd obviously been asleep; there were crease marks from the cushion on her cheek and her spectacular eyes were a bit foggy. Taking advantage of her confusion, he quickly established that Olivia was sleeping over at Mama B's and that Bay was, blissfully, alone.

And a plan started to form.

He'd been on his way to Muzi's; they'd made vague plans to hit some bars, maybe a club or two. Needing a hit of adrenaline, he decided to take his bike, even if it meant he couldn't drink for the rest of the night. But instead of heading to Muzi's flat in Camps Bay, his bike found itself—strange, that!—on Bay's street, and then he was knocking on her door...

He'd invited her out for a ride and she'd hemmed and hawed and then hemmed and hawed some more. After promising that he wouldn't stop anywhere where he would be recognized or, worse, photographed—a complete novelty because his dates tended to want to be seen on his arm—she finally agreed to join him.

At that point he hadn't had a destination in mind but, on hearing that Bay preferred casual and very low-key, an idea occurred. While waiting for her to change—he'd told her to wear jeans and flat boots—he'd texted Muzi and told him that he was heading for Kwezi's if he wanted to join them.

Muzi might or might not; either way it was sure to be a fun night out. He was with Bay, how could it not be? And best of all, their destination, he was sure, would surprise Bay. She wouldn't expect him to take her into the heart of Gugulethu, one of Cape Town's oldest townships. Hell, he'd never expected to take a woman there either. He couldn't think of a single woman he'd ever dated who wouldn't wrinkle her pretty nose at the thought of joining working-class folks at a working-class place. His dates expected haute, innovative cuisine and extensive wine lists, not barbecued meat and cheap beer.

Bay had spoken a little about her travels, how she always sought out the places where the locals ate, and he knew she wasn't squeamish or snobby. Bay, he'd come to realize, didn't give a rat's ass about expensive champagne and modern cuisine, about seeing and, more important, being seen.

In fact, she'd told him, quite emphatically, that she did not want to appear in any social column. Ever.

Luckily, he'd never encountered a reporter, photographer or any of Cape Town's A-listers at Kwezi's Tavern. Kwezi's was his, Radd's and Muzi's secret, the place they headed to when they wanted complete anonymity.

He could've, Digby thought as he took the off-ramp and stopped at a traffic light, left

Bay at home and met Muzi here on his own but...

But the hell of it was that he enjoyed Bay, liked her company. She was a great designer and had a fantastic work ethic, but she was also quick and witty and thoughtful. And so damn sexy he frequently forgot to breathe.

Digby tightened his grip on the throttle and sighed. What had he been thinking when he suggested that she be in control of their going-to-bed timing? God, he hoped she caved soon because not having her was driving him crap-bat insane. When he wasn't having his Radd dying dreams, he dreamed of her naked and writhing and he frequently woke up at the crucial moment, hard as a rock and groaning. Sleep, never easy, had become something he started to dread.

He really had to start getting his attraction to her under control. Yeah, he liked her, adored her body, couldn't wait to get her into bed but...

But that was it.

He didn't believe in love, didn't want it in his life. He couldn't see himself ever having what Radd did with Brin. He couldn't imag-

ine himself engaged or being in a commit-
ted relationship. First, he'd been on his own,
doing his thing, for a damn long time and
didn't think he could change now, but more
than that, he didn't want to...

He wasn't brave enough. He knew what it
felt like to have love and then to lose it, to feel
like he was being ripped apart. Why would
he ever put himself in that position again?

No, the sooner he and Bay slept together,
the sooner he could get her out of his system.
The sooner he could move on and return to
his normal life.

So, genius, let me ask you this...

The light turned green and Digby tried to
ignore the sarcastic voice coming from deep
in his soul.

*If sex is all you want, then why didn't you
stay in her empty house and try to seduce her
there? Why is she on your bike? Why are you
taking her to one of your favorite places in
the world? The place that you've never, ever
taken a girl before?*

Good questions and, annoyingly, not ones
he had answers to.

* * *

From the minute she climbed on the back of Digby's bike, Bay cursed herself for accepting his invitation out, terrified that, despite his promise, he'd take her somewhere where he'd be recognized, where someone would photograph them together.

If that happened, she might put her custody of Liv in jeopardy, and Bay mentally kicked herself. She'd started to, fifteen times, maybe more, ask Digby to take her home, but on his bike, their faces hidden by the black helmets and visors, they were unrecognizable. And she loved flying down the highway, the warm wind whipping her cotton shirt, confident in Digby's handling of the monstrously powerful bike.

She'd see where they ended up, she decided, and if she felt that there was the slightest chance of recognition, she'd ask Digby to take her home. And he would, she knew that for sure.

But of all the places to eat in the city, she hadn't expected to arrive at a colorful tavern in Gugulethu. There were plastic tables and chairs outside the restaurant, filled with jovial patrons tucking into mounds of barbecued meat.

Inside the tavern, rows of wooden tables left little space to walk, and to one side sat a bank of display fridges. Inside the fridges were plastic tubs of meat, waiting to be cooked on open fire behind the restaurant. Digby, after greeting the owner and the man behind the display case, ordered steak and ribs, a soda for himself and beer for Bay. He asked after Muzi but was told he hadn't arrived yet.

The tables were full to bursting and Bay wondered where they'd sit, but Kwezi, the owner, led them to the middle of the room and booted two teenagers out of their seats. When Bay protested, he waved her words away, telling her that they were young, they would survive. She and Digby sat down in the middle of what was a jolly party and were instantly welcomed by the other customers at the table. Nobody, she was sure, knew who Digby was and if they did, they didn't care.

Bay was completely surprised at how at ease he, a multibillionaire, was in this working-class restaurant. Despite having eaten in the best eateries in the world, owning one himself, he didn't seem to care that the plates were mismatched, that there wasn't a wine menu or servers. He was also perfectly content to wait in line for his meat to be cooked, to eat with his fingers.

Her boss, the lover in her dreams, was anything but a snob. His lack of entitlement and ability to talk to anybody anywhere made him, if it was at all possible, even more attractive in her eyes.

She hadn't thought that was possible but here she was, falling a little deeper...

After eating more meat than she normally did in a month and drinking a few beers and laughing at the quips of the middle-aged couple to her right, Bay leaned her shoulder into Digby's and turned her head to smile at him. "Having fun?" he asked.

"So much fun," Bay replied. "This was not how I expected to spend Friday night. I wanted to be at home, relaxing, but I'm here and I feel like I *am* at home. And I am so relaxed."

"That could also be the three beers you've had," Digby told her on a lazy grin.

Bay wrinkled her nose before shaking her head. "Seriously, thank you for bringing me here. I've eaten street food and local dishes on five continents, but I've never visited a traditional African tavern before. The meat is awesome."

Digby popped another piece of steak into his mouth and grinned. When he finished chewing, he picked up her beer and took a swig. He looked longingly at her bottle and when Bay suggested he order his own, he shook his head. "I'm going to be in control of a superpowerful machine in a couple of hours and I can't afford to have my judgment impaired. Especially since I have a gorgeous passenger I'm responsible for."

Bay showed him her appreciation by dropping a kiss on his lips. Before she was tempted to take their embrace further, she pulled back. "Thank you for that."

Digby turned to face her, his elbow on the table. "Are you still okay to work tomorrow?"

Bay nodded. "Why wouldn't I be?"

Digby pushed a strand of hair off her forehead, his fingertip light on her skin. Yet she still quivered. Bay was starting to think that she could be ninety, having experienced a lifetime of Digby's caresses, and she'd still respond like this. "Tomorrow is Saturday, you've been working like a demon and you deserve a day off, to sleep in."

"My boss is a hard taskmaster—he's been working me to the bone," Bay teased. When Digby didn't respond to her teasing, she allowed her fingers to drift over the back of his broad hand. "I'm fine, Digby. A little tired maybe but we need to press on ahead or else we won't get the ballroom done in time for your foundation's ball in two months."

Digby grimaced, moving his hand to wind his fingers through hers. "Fair point." He thought for a moment before speaking again. "I'm just so sick of the four walls of my office...why don't we work out of my house tomorrow?"

She was also getting cabin fever so she quickly nodded. Okay, truthfully, she also wanted to see where Digby lived. And, because his house was within The Vane's grounds, she didn't have to worry about being spied on, least of all by nosy reporters. She nodded. "Nine-ish?"

"Perfect," Digby said, squeezing her fingers before pulling away to turn his attention back to his food.

Bay, marveling at how much he could eat, changed the subject. "Now, tell me, how do you know Kwezi? Is he another of your friends from your smart boarding school?"

Digby shook his head. "Kwezi's dad was a foreman on our vineyard and we've known each other since we were kids. He, Radd and I spent a lot of time together between the ages of six and thirteen. Then his father was hurt in a tractor accident and they moved back to the city and we lost touch until ten or so years ago."

Bay placed her elbow on the table and her chin in the palm of her hand. "And how did you reconnect?"

Digby saw Kwezi standing at a nearby table and motioned him over. "Bay wants to know how we reconnected, dude."

Kwezi asked a customer to scoot up so that he could sit down opposite Bay. He took a long sip of water from the bottle in his hand. "Digby was playing rugby for his university. I was playing for a local club. We met again on the field. I gave him a concussion that knocked him out cold."

Kwezi, as Bay had already noticed, was a huge guy, six-four or six-five, all muscle. Being tackled by him would be the equivalent of being run over by a tank. "What? *Really?*"

Kwezi shrugged, not at all remorseful. "Not my fault he's weak."

"It was a high tackle." Digby pointed a rib at him.

"High tackle my ass," Kwezi stated. He looked at Bay and shook his head. "Your boy couldn't take the heat."

"You did go on to play topflight rugby, dude," Digby grumbled, but Bay saw the amusement in his eyes. He looked so very relaxed, so at ease in this casual restaurant. It was a good look on him.

Looking at Bay, Digby continued his explanation. "Kwezi was on track to play for our national team but his mom fell ill and needed help with his siblings, so he came back here and opened up this tavern."

Kwezi reached across the table and snagged a rib from Digby's plate. Holding it in his enormous fingers, he bit down, chewed and looked thoughtful.

"I'm thinking about expanding—there are premises across town I think would be good for another tavern."

Digby pushed his plate away and wiped his hands on a paper napkin. "You sound hesitant."

Kwezi lifted one enormous shoulder. "Money is tight out there and unemployment is skyrocketing. I'm not sure if there is enough money in the system to sustain another tavern."

"That's what you said when we first discussed you opening up this place—no money, high unemployment, too much competition." Digby made a show of looking around the packed-with-people joint. "It looks like you are doing okay.

"Trust your instincts, bruh," Digby told him. "They were spot-on back then—they are sharper now."

Bay—who'd been watching the intricate moves of a young, gorgeous dark-skinned woman on the makeshift dance floor in the far corner of the room, her hips shimmying and her braids flying—pulled her attention back to Digby when he stood up abruptly. Holding his hand out to Bay, Digby nodded to the full dance floor. "Do you want to dance?"

Bay cocked her head to listen to the music, feeling the deep bass lines reverberating through her body. Like the tavern, the music was rough and raw and wholly authentic.

She nodded, stood up, placed her hand in Digby's and smiled. "Yes, please." She turned to Kwezi and excused herself. "I hope to see you again."

Kwezi left his seat and walked around the table. He gave Bay a brief hug and a wide grin. His dark eyes twinkled with mischief. "Digby dances nearly as well as he plays rugby," he pulled a face and shuddered theatrically, "so if you need someone to show you some moves, I'll be around."

Digby's shoulder bumped Kwezi's in retaliation and Bay couldn't help laughing when Digby failed to move him at all.

Bay led Digby to the crowded dance floor, enjoying the rhythmic beat of Kwaito music pumping at full blast from the massive speakers on either side of the makeshift space. She felt the beat in her feet, in her heart, deep in her soul. Hitting the dance floor, she turned to face Digby, noticing that they'd been separated by a couple getting down and a little dirty. Not waiting for Digby to join her, she lifted her hands and instinctively started to move with the beat, shimmying her hips and rolling her shoulders, turning on the spot, her hair flying.

Dancing made her feel sexy and sensual and hot, and the African rhythm connected her to her country and its people. As she waited for Digby to join her, Bay wondered whether he could really dance. Like all women, she found men with rhythm incredibly sexy.

But even if Digby couldn't dance, his willingness to dance with her without caring what anyone thought was pretty damn cool. She liked guys who were carefree enough, confident enough to look let go, have some fun, not caring whether they appeared silly or not.

And Digby had confidence in spades.

As it turned out, Digby was a very good dancer and came off as anything but silly.

On reaching her spot in the middle of the floor, he placed a hand on her hip, his thigh between hers, and immediately started to move in time to the beat. His eyes slammed into hers and in all that blue she saw desire and need.

Bay, conscious that she held all his attention—such a turn on!—caught his small grin before he was gripping her hand, spinning her out, to pull her back into his chest, then leading her into an empty space with a quick, confident shuffle.

He spun her out again and let her go and Bay instinctively realized that, while he was an excellent dancer, he wanted to spotlight her, that this was her moment, her chance to let loose and fly. Shaking off the last of her inhibitions, Bay fell into the music, allowing instinct to take over. She shimmied and shook, twisted and turned, knowing that whatever she did, wherever she was, Digby was there, urging her on, to let go, to dip and swirl, to allow the music to carry her away. Sometimes he held her, most times he allowed her space to move on her own but he was there...

Always there.

She was the picture; he was the frame. Dance

was emotion in motion and she reveled in every note, every beat, understanding the lyrics even though she didn't understand the language. As she moved, she flirted with Digby, with herself, with life in general and God...

She felt so very alive.

After three fast songs, the track switched to a song that was slow and sensual and, without hesitation, Bay moved into Digby's arms, looping one arm around his neck and placing her other hand above his heart, enjoying the steady thump-bump under her fingers. His hands rested low on her back, just above the curve of her ass, keeping her anchored to him, his hard erection pushing into her hip. They swayed in place, still flirting without words, seducing in silence.

Dancing was, as someone far cleverer than she once noted, "the vertical expression of a horizontal urge."

Indeed...

CHAPTER SIX

THE NEXT MORNING, a few minutes after she left Olivia with Roisin—the two were off to the beach today—Bay followed Digby's directions to his house. She ambled to the back of the property, through the impressive flower and vegetable garden, another rose garden and across a swath of lawn, to a double-story structure right at the back of the parcel, as far away from the guests as she could possibly be on the huge acreage. Feeling the sun on her bare shoulders, she stopped at the end of the path and looked up, sighing at the incredible view of Table Mountain. Today the mountain loomed over the tract, so close she felt like she could reach out and touch its crags and slopes.

She had, she admitted, a bit of a hangover, not helped by too little sleep and a few beers. She'd had so much fun with Digby last night.

But, admittedly, she'd been very disappointed when, somewhere around three in the morning, Digby dropped her off at her cottage. He'd kept his distance and when she tried to kiss him, he told her she was a little drunk, tired and that she needed sleep more than she needed sex.

He'd been wrong there and she'd been prepared to argue but Digby told her that, while he wanted her more than he wanted his heart to keep beating, it wasn't the right moment.

He didn't want her to have any regrets, to be able to say that alcohol lowered her inhibitions, that her ability to make good decisions was affected. If she wanted to sleep with him, she could just say the word, but preferably when she was completely sober.

Digby was, despite his reputation, a gentleman. Damn him.

Bay slipped her sunglasses onto her face, passed through a small grove of trees and lifted her eyebrows as she approached a large stone building. Digby had informed her that he'd only recently moved into this converted stone barn; up until a few months back he'd been using one of the larger of the hotel suites as his primary residence.

She couldn't pretend; Bay was eager to see his home.

Bay touched the wall of the barn, admiring the work of the stonemasons. Needing to see more, she hurried around the side and placed her hand on her heart when she noticed the monochromatic glass windows rising from the floor to the pitch of the roof, opening up the entire house to the view.

Fabulous. Good job, architects.

Seeing that one of the sliding doors was open, Bay rapped on the frame and stepped inside, straight into the huge open floor space. A freestanding fireplace stood in the center of the room, with a spacious lounge on one side and a dining area on the other. Beyond the eight-seater table with dining chairs upholstered in rich jewel colors was a sleek, gourmet kitchen.

Entranced, Bay looked up. A set of spiral stairs on each side of the barn provided access to what she presumed to be the master bedroom and a guest bedroom on the mezzanine level, with a thin walkway against the back wall joining the two rooms. The ancient beams of the structure were exposed, and light poured in from skylights above.

"I'm in love," she murmured.

"I presume you are talking about my house and not me."

Bay turned to see Digby lying on the couch behind her, her breath hitching when she saw he was only wearing running shorts and sneakers on his feet. Taking a moment, she admired his gorgeous body, the light sprinkling of hair on his chest, the ridges of his muscular stomach and those gorgeous hip muscles disappearing into his shorts. The bicep muscle of the arm resting over his eyes was hard and impressive. God, he was physically powerful and stupendously sexy.

Down, girl.

Digby pushed himself to his feet and gestured to the kitchen. "I'm going to take a quick shower and then we can get to work. Make yourself comfortable, help yourself to coffee, whatever you want."

Bay nodded. "Do you mind if I explore?"

"Not at all." Digby walked to the closest stairs before jogging up the steep curves to his bedroom. Bay dropped her bag, laptop case and art satchel on the dining room table and wandered into the kitchen, peeking into a pantry and beyond that, a utility room. Backtracking, she saw another door at the end of the room and opened it to reveal a smaller lounge complete with huge couches, a massive flat screen and speakers everywhere. There was an interconnecting door that led to a study, lined with shelves. A huge desk was pushed to the wall and held files and expensive-looking computer equipment.

The office's second door opened back onto the main living area and from there she walked up the spiral staircase and onto the landing outside the spare bedroom. It was the standard double-bed guest room with en suite shower, perfectly decorated but, in her opinion, a little bland.

Bay thought about going back downstairs but she was curious, so she walked across the narrow landing thirty feet above the living room below and ended up outside Digby's room. The stairs were to her right and she should use them, but his bedroom door was open and she wanted a quick look. His bedroom had glass on two sides and Bay could easily imagine him waking up every morning in that enormous bed, covered with plain white linen, and rolling over to look at the city's favorite landmark.

Amazing.

Then her view improved considerably when Digby walked across her line of sight, with only a towel wrapped around his waist, his hair wet and droplets of water running down his tanned shoulders.

His body was even nicer to look at than the view outside and that was saying a hell of a lot...

She should go before he saw her, should walk down those stairs. But Bay's feet were glued to the landing and she knew she wasn't going anywhere...

"You're welcome to come inside but, I have to warn you, if you do, I'm going to do my best to tempt you into getting naked," Digby said, turning around to look at her.

Her eyes slammed into his and a million thoughts bombarded her. He was keeping his word; sleeping with him would still be her decision, her choice.

She should go...

She wanted to stay...

She was playing with fire...

But she wanted to burn...

The past six months had been all about Olivia, about doing what she had to do, what she'd promised to do. She couldn't remember one occasion lately, apart from last night, when she'd done something for herself, spoiled herself in any way. She hadn't bought new clothes, gone out to eat or clubbing. Her entire focus had been on Olivia and nursing her through this catastrophic change in her life and dealing with her own grief.

She loved Olivia, she *did*, but wasn't she allowed, just once, to spoil herself?

And sleeping with Digby would be a hell of a treat. He would be a memory she'd have for the rest of her life.

She liked him, was crazy attracted to him, and she'd love to learn all he had to teach her. They were both single and unattached and best of all—no one would ever know.

Digby must've seen the capitulation on her face because he smiled and gently ordered her to come to him. Bay hesitated, but only for a moment. Then, with a tiny shrug, she stepped into his room, walking around the huge bed to stop in front of him. Digby lifted his hands to hold her face and he gently rubbed his nose against hers, his mouth curved into a smile.

"I'll go slow and if you change your mind at any point, just tell me and I'll stop, okay? And there will be no hard feelings."

Bay bit her lip. "Promise?"

"I promise. You're in control here, sweetheart. We'll go as far as you feel comfortable with."

Yeah, as she'd noted last night, under all that charm, Digby was a gentleman, a man with honor.

Reassured, Bay placed her palms on his bare chest, sighing at his smooth, masculine skin. Needing him, she put her hand behind his neck and pulled his head down to reach his lips with hers. "Will you kiss me, Dig?"

"Abso-freaking-lutely," Digby muttered, covering her mouth with his. Bay instantly opened her lips, allowing his tongue to slide against hers. She couldn't help moving closer and pushed her breasts into his chest, wishing she could step inside him, to know him from the inside out. Digby's hands skated up her back and then burrowed under her sleeveless top to find bare skin. After many minutes of thought-and-reason-stealing kisses—or was it hours, since time no longer had any meaning?—Digby pulled back to rest his temple on hers. "You have far too many clothes on, darling."

She knew that he was asking for permission to carry on so, instead of speaking—she doubted her brain's ability to form words—Bay stepped away from him and reached for the button of her shorts. After pulling down the zip, she allowed the garment to fall down her hips to the floor, leaving her standing in her T-shirt and panties.

"Gorgeous," Digby said, on a low whistle. And at that moment, Bay did feel lovely, appreciated, even a little adored.

It gave her the courage to continue so she crisscrossed her arms, gripped her shirt and slowly pulled it up her chest, revealing her rather prosaic sports bra.

She glanced down and grimaced. "If I knew that we were going to be doing this today, I would've worn something sexier."

Digby shook his head as his eyes traveled

up her long legs to her breasts, to her face and down again. "You could be wearing the sexiest, most expensive lingerie known to man and I'd barely notice. All my attention is on the present, not the packaging. I'm taking in your incredibly smooth skin, that incredible shape of your legs—" his hand stroked her hip and slid around to palm her butt "—and you have the most perfect ass I've ever seen."

That had to be a lie—he'd dated models and actresses—but she wasn't about to argue. And she wouldn't spoil this moment by comparing herself to his previous liaisons. That way madness lay.

She wanted Digby to drive her out of her mind but not like that!

"Take off your bra, Bay," Digby commanded, and Bay stepped back to lift it up and over her head, feeling a little self-conscious when Digby stared at her chest. She wasn't a C or D cup, hell, on good days she was barely a B cup. But the admiration in Digby's eyes was hard to miss and he groaned when his thumb skated across her nipple, making it pebble.

"Beautiful," Digby murmured, bending his head to suck her into his mouth. Bay held his head in her hands, moaning with pleasure as he sucked her to the point of pain, before lifting his head to blow on her bud. Then his gentle tongue soothed the tiny sting.

So, so good.

Digby dropped to his knees to place kisses on her flat stomach, dipped his tongue into her belly button and eased her panties down her hips. He nuzzled his nose into her thin strip of hair before going lower, then lower still.

Bay sank into his caresses, utterly comfortable with the intimate act. She trusted him, she thought. Trusted him with every inch of her body, knowing that he'd never hurt her, or push her beyond what she felt comfortable doing. Then, as pleasure began to build and he did something amazing with his tongue, all thoughts faded and she concentrated on the enjoyment only he could give her.

But she didn't want ecstasy to be one-sided, not this first time, so she urged him to his feet and pulled his towel from his body. She licked a bead of moisture off his chest and lifted her eyes to his as her hand encircled his erection.

"I'm not on any birth control so I'm really, really hoping you have condoms," Bay told him, dropping butterfly kisses on his chest.

In her hand Digby hardened again—how was that possible?—and he released a small groan. "I do."

Bay nodded and looked at the bed.

Digby dropped a hard, sexy kiss on her mouth before lifting her in his arms and all but throwing her onto it. She laughed and her breath caught at the sapphire-blue color of his eyes, burning with lust, desire and what she hoped might be affection.

Digby walked up the staircase, carefully carrying a tray, Bay's cell phone tucked under his arm. Nudging open the door to the bedroom, he found Bay sitting on the window seat in his room, hair wet from the shower and wearing one of his T-shirts, her legs tucked up underneath her. Seeing her there, sitting in the muted sunlight, she looked so…

When no other word would do, he eventually acknowledged the only word that did…

She looked and felt…

Right.

And that scared him senseless.

Digby placed the tray on the bench at the end of the bed and, unable to resist, bent down to drop a kiss on Bay's wet head, still able to pick up traces of her citrus-and-jasmine scent underneath the masculine smell of his shower soap. Casual affection wasn't something he engaged in so he had no idea where this need to touch her came from.

Bay sent him a smile and took the phone he held out to her. "Roisin called," he told her.

Her body immediately tensed, her hand flying up to her chest, and alarm jumped in and out of her eyes. "Oh, God, really? Is everything okay? Is Olivia okay? What did she want?"

"She's fine, Bay, really. She just called because Liv wanted to tell you that she saw the penguins at Boulders Beach. Liv also informed me that she wants to bring one home. She's convinced it would be quite happy living in the biggest of The Vane's pools."

Her panic subsided but her hand remained on her chest. "Olivia spoke to you? On the phone?"

He nodded and pushed the bench seat closer

to the window so that they could reach the tray of coffee and pastries he'd ordered from room service. "She asked to speak to you. I told her you were in the bathroom, not a lie, and she was happy to babble away. I heard about sand castles and birds and that Roisin bought her an ice cream."

For someone who didn't want children, and didn't know how to deal with them, some sort of rapport was growing between him and Olivia. He didn't seem to be able to resist her and that was, for him, unusual in the extreme.

Digby comforted himself with the thought that he doubted many people in the world could resist Miss Olivia. She was, at three, a force of nature, and he was thankful he wouldn't have to guide her through the teenage years. He was not that brave.

Give her thirty years, Digby decided, and Olivia would be President of the World.

Digby lifted Bay's legs and sat down, placing her legs across his thighs, as she reached for a Danish and then bit down. Her eyes widened as she chewed and a look of bliss crossed her face.

"So, so good," she mumbled taking another huge bite.

Digby smiled, enjoying the look of pleasure on her face as she finished the pastry. "My pastry chef is world-class."

"I'd say," Bay replied.

He reached for a cup of coffee and handed it to her, smiling as she wrapped her hands around the mug. She'd had the same look of anticipation on her face when she wrapped her hands around his erection earlier. Digby sighed, felt the action in his pants and told himself to stand down. They'd made love twice and fooled around again in the shower; he needed some time to recover and so did Bay.

But damn, it had been the best sex of his life. How had that happened?

Forcing his thoughts from how they'd loved each other and how right—that word again!—it felt, Digby turned his thoughts back to Olivia. "You're an amazing mom, Bay," he quietly told her, reaching for his own mug. "If I had said there was a problem, I imagine you would've been out that door in a flash."

"Of course I would," Bay replied. "That's

what moms do. Or even what aunts, trying to be moms, do."

He knew that wasn't true. "Not all mothers, Bay. I should know."

"What do you mean?"

Digby grimaced, wishing he hadn't opened this door. Then again, with Bay, the doors he normally kept locked seemed to spring open without any help from him.

He looked at her curious face and knew he was going to tell her. He couldn't not. Bay was his truth serum. "When I was twelve, I suffered an injury on the rugby field and was rushed to hospital in an ambulance— they were worried about my neck. The coach called my mom, who happened to be in the country at the time. She was at the family farm, our vineyard, not twenty minutes away from where I was playing. She told my coach to let her know if something more serious developed. Jack was the one to rush to my side."

Bay looked at him, aghast. "That is truly shocking."

Digby shrugged and looked out the window, idly noticing that his private lap pool was full of leaves, and made a mental note to remind the maintenance crew to have it cleaned. "It was just the way she was."

"And your dad?"

"He followed my mom's lead." Digby told himself to stop talking but his mouth was on a mission of its own. "You've got to understand—my parents didn't engage with us, me in particular. They were very over having kids by the time I came along."

Bay frowned. "They could've chosen not to have any more kids after Jack was born. I mean, I'm glad they didn't, obviously, but that was a choice they could've made. They had their heir, why have more kids?"

Digby wasn't sure whether to tell her that the reason he was born came down to hard, cold cash. Would she understand? Would she recoil away, and would her disgust taint him? Taint what they'd just shared?

He hesitated and Bay put a hand on his arm. "Digby? What is it?"

Despite his hesitation about sharing something so private, the words came tumbling out. "The Tempest-Vanes weren't good at stocking the family tree and my father was the sole Tempest-Vane heir. My great-grandfather told my father he'd give him two million for every male child he produced. Three boys resulted in a hefty paycheck."

Bay looked, as he expected, shocked. "That's dreadful. And if you'd been a girl?"

Digby shrugged. "No money if that's what you are asking."

"Wow, that's a superb example of misogyny," Bay commented. "Your parents weren't very likable, were they?"

Now, that was the understatement of the century. Sometimes he actively hated them for being so damn selfish, so reckless, so impossibly self-centered. For leaving them to raise themselves. His biggest dream, as a kid, was having two parents who put him and his brothers first, who gave them both roots and wings and were a soft place to fall when things went wrong. But he'd never had that. As a result, he didn't know how a family worked and couldn't see himself giving a family the things he most needed as a kid. And if he couldn't do it properly, he wouldn't do it at all.

So, no family for him.

"Radd and I were definitely surplus to what

was required. Zia had no interest in us at all and she frequently told the press that she wasn't cut out for motherhood."

He'd repeated her words to reporters, saying he wasn't cut out for a family, but the difference between them was that he wasn't a father and his kids couldn't read what he said about them online or in the papers.

Bay's soft hand stroked the ball of his shoulder and her touch calmed him. It was so strange that, when he spoke about his parents to her, the subject didn't sting as much as it normally did.

"Did you see much of her growing up?" Bay asked softly, waiting for him to continue.

Digby placed his hand on her thigh and drew patterns in her soft skin with his thumb. "When I was about ten, there was a stretch when I didn't see either Gil or Zia for about six months. They went to the States for an extended holiday and didn't return."

"But your dad was running Tempest-Vane at that time."

"Running? No. Looting the company of all its assets? Hell, yes," Digby stated. He turned, moving his legs so that they were on either side of Bay's legs, lifting her calves to rest on his thighs. He smiled when she rearranged his T-shirt to cover her intimate area. It wasn't like he hadn't explored her from tip to toe but he wasn't going to embarrass her by mentioning that. And he liked her modesty, it was a nice change from models who had no inhibition at all.

"I suppose they are the reason why I was, am, such an attention hound," Digby said. He'd never said that to anyone before and couldn't believe that he'd voiced such an intimate thought to Bay. Next, he'd be telling her about his nightmare and his dread of Radd dying. The dream had visited again last night, harder and deeper and darker than normal. But instead of seeing Radd's face in that coffin, the features and body had been indistinct. And scary as hell.

Bay placed the last bite of Danish on the side plate and her coffee mug on the tray. After wiping her fingers with a linen napkin, she placed her hands on his knees and squeezed. "Will you explain that remark, Dig?"

He knew that if he changed the subject

she would respect his need for privacy and he considered doing exactly that. Then he saw the sympathy in her eyes and shrugged. "They never gave me any attention so I looked for it everywhere I could. At school, I excelled at sports and worked hard at it because those guys were recognized and acknowledged, respected. I became the class clown because making people laugh was attention. After Jack died, I acted out because any attention, good or bad, was better than none at all."

He'd admitted so much this morning already—would he regret his loquaciousness later?—so he might as well tell her the rest. "When I left school, I went to the university and nobody cared who I was or what I did. There were so many kids there and I felt more lost than ever before—every day I felt like I was jumping out of my skin. So, in the few moments I had between studying and setting up our internet security company, I chased adrenaline. And I loved it, it allowed me to get out of my head."

Bay threaded her fingers through his and simply waited for him to continue.

"Somehow the crazy stunts I did started to attract attention, press attention, and I liked that. I liked reading about myself in the papers—it was an acknowledgment, you know?"

Bay nodded.

"I was called the wild Tempest-Vane, the fun brother, more like his parents than the brilliant Jack and introverted Radd."

Bay tipped her head to the side. "I suppose that after you sold your company, the tech one, and you became instabillionaires, the press attention skyrocketed."

Digby nodded. "Yeah, that was a crazy time. Every date I went on, every function I attended, was covered. According to the tabloid press, I was engaged twice, secretly married once and have a couple of secret babies." Digby heard the bitterness in his voice and closed his eyes, mortified. "The women who dated me enjoyed the exposure—many of them translated their brief moment of fame into careers as reality stars, actresses and models."

"Did it annoy you that they used you?" Bay asked.

"I guess it just got boring. Although, I was pissed when one snuck a photographer onto the hotel's grounds and he hid out in the bushes and snapped a photo of her topless in the sunshine."

"Yeah, I saw that photo," Bay said.

Digby winced. Of course she had. He cursed.

"He got a great snap of your hand on her breast," Bay pointed out. He pulled a face, uncomfortable at the reminder.

"The press taking photos of me at functions and in public places is something I can handle—it's part of the deal of being a Tempest-Vane. But her invading my privacy, bringing someone into my home, was unacceptable."

"Damn right," Bay agreed. After a moment's silence, she asked another question. "Is that a warning? To me?"

Digby took a moment to connect the dots, to work out what she meant. He shook his head, a touch more violently than he normally did. "No! Hell! I never thought that for a moment!"

"Okay."

He could see a trace of skepticism in her

eye but then she turned her gaze off him to look out the window. Since she was keeping her eyes on the view, he felt her retreat and cursed himself for being insensitive. *Way to go, Tempest-Vane, you fool.*

"Tell me about your relationships with your parents," Digby said, wanting to engage her again. "I bet you were showered with affection and attention."

Pain flashed across her fine features and her shoulders tensed. He thought she wouldn't answer but then she released a heavy sigh. "I was showered with attention and affection until I went to high school. Then everything changed."

"What happened?" Digby asked, refilling his coffee mug.

"I left my expensive, small, insulated primary school on a scholarship to Foresters..."

The exclusive girls-only school in Paarl? Yeah, he knew the school and was impressed that she'd won a scholarship to the prestigious institution. "Did you hate it?"

"No, I loved it. But I was exposed to new people, different views, and I embraced the diversity of the school. Within a couple of months, I'd been exposed to new ideas and literature and I had to confront, and deal with the notion, that my parents, especially my father, were narrow-minded, misogynistic, homophobic and ridiculously conservative.

"Worst of all, I realized that they were also full-blown racists," she added.

Digby winced.

Bay ran a hand over her face, her eyes darker with pain. "Yeah. I challenged them and they pushed back. I refused to back down, and my father became irrationally angry. He's old-school, he believes his word is the law and his are the only opinions that matter. I'm not sure what annoyed him more, that I was calling him out or that I had an opinion different to his.

"Before I went to high school, he was affectionate and loving. We were exceptionally close and I idolized him. After I started challenging him, his attitude toward me changed and he became, well, mean. And nothing I said could sway him. Just made it worse. And when he realized that I wouldn't back down and that he couldn't intimidate me into changing my views, he pulled away and started to ignore or ridicule me. I went from being dad-dy's girl to being a pariah in my own home. By the time I was sixteen, we could barely greet each other."

Digby wished he could hug, or love, all her pain away. "I'm so sorry, sweetheart."

"My mom told me to stop rocking the boat, to just agree with him but I couldn't— I couldn't condone what he was saying," Bay explained, her whiskey-colored eyes murky with unshed tears. "After years of either him screaming at me or flat-out ignoring me, I left home, went to the university, again on a scholarship, and we didn't have much to do or say to each other. Layla followed me to the same uni and those were the happiest years of our lives. She met Ali there and they were so in love. She couldn't tell our parents that she was dating a mixed-race, Muslim man. She still had a relationship with my parents."

Digby waited, knowing there was more.

"My parents surprised us at our flat early one morning. They rang the doorbell. I opened the door to them, half-asleep. Layla came stumbling out of her bedroom, quickly followed by Ali, and you didn't need an interpreter to know what they'd been doing."

"And the crap hit the fan."

Bay nodded. "Big time." Bay closed her eyes and Digby knew that her memories were still fresh. "My dad turned on me and blamed everything on me and my radical education and liberal views. If I had just stayed home, been a good girl, content with the status quo, none of this would've happened."

Digby noticed the sheen of tears in her eyes and gently plucked her from her seat and cuddled her against his chest, kissing her hair as he did. God, parents were supposed to love their kids, not rip them apart.

"After telling us that we were dead to them, they left and Layla was gutted. I was angry and horrified and embarrassed and so, so sad. But Ali was so cool. He just picked up Layla, told her his family was hers and that they would be happy. And they were, they really, really were."

"I'm glad that they found each other," Digby said, lifting his lips off her hair to say the words.

"I am too. Anyway, Ali's family is now mine too." Bay used the balls of her hands to wipe the tears from her face. She sniffed, took a sip of coffee from his mug and scooted off his lap. She walked over to the second wall of windows, folded her arms and stared at the mountain, watching the tablecloth settle over the previously clear top.

Her next words were a bombshell he didn't expect.

"They want Olivia, Dig."

Her words were flat and cold and he couldn't make sense of them. "What? What do you mean they want Olivia? *Who* wants her?"

"My parents are applying for custody of her and are going to tell the court that I'm unfit to raise her. They have money, they are still young, they are only in their midfifties and they have experience raising children." Bay tried to smile. "It's a good argument."

Digby struggled to digest this new information. He stood up and walked over to her, noting her pale face. "But she's mixed race. And you said that he's a racist."

Bay sent him a wan smile. "Ah, they'll ignore that inconvenient fact. But I'm terrified they'll raise her as they raised us, to be a good wife and daughter, to not have her own opinions, to believe that a man's opinion is more important than hers will ever be. And if I lose her, Layla will haunt me forever."

"You're not going to lose her, sweetheart," Digby told her, his hands reaching for hers. "Layla and her husband gave you guardianship—the court will take that into account."

"God, I hope so. But the fact remains that I have no child-rearing experience and I've spent the last few years bouncing around the world. I'm also self-employed and my income stream isn't long-term steady."

"I think you are borrowing trouble, honey. I think you have an excellent shot of retaining custody."

When her eyes connected with his, Digby knew he wasn't going to like what she was about to say. "Unlike your previous girlfriends, Digby, you don't have to worry about me using you to up my visibility. In fact, my worst nightmare would be us hitting the gossip columns—I cannot tell you how much I'd hate that."

She removed her hands from his and wrapped her arms around her waist. She briefly closed her eyes and her chest rose and fell; her agitation was obvious. "I can't be linked, in any way, to you, Digby. It might hurt my chances to keep custody of Olivia."

Digby felt like she'd shoved a knife into his chest. "What? *Why?*"

"My lawyer says my judgment might be called into question if they—my parents or the press—discover that I'm dating or sleeping with you." Bay bit her lip, her shoulders lifting to reach her ears. "You've led a bit of a wild life and…well…"

"Just spit it out, Bay," Digby said, his voice cool. He knew what was coming—he'd been here before, taking on the sins of his parents. But, damn, it had never stung this much before…

Bay sucked in a deep breath and her words rushed out. "Some people think you are like your parents and, obviously, they'd wonder what effect you'd have on Olivia if you were to become a permanent fixture in my life. I told my lawyer that you are anticommitment, that nothing like that would happen, but she says that it doesn't matter, that perception is all that's important."

"I'm not like my parents, Bay, not when it comes to the important stuff," Digby said, his voice stiff with annoyance. God, he hoped she didn't hear the hint of hurt under his irritation.

"I know that, Digby, but the judge and lawyers don't. And I can't take the chance of losing her, Dig." In her eyes, he saw defiance and determination and knew that whatever they had was now lost, that the spark between them had been doused. "This is Olivia's life we are talking about—I cannot take any risks that might backfire."

"So you have to choose between her and me," Digby said, his tone frigid. Would anyone ever put him first? Then the wave of shame broke over his head when he remembered that Olivia was innocent, a child, and he was an adult with a crapload of resources.

Bay looked sad but resolute. "This isn't about choosing, Digby. What I said was that I can't be romantically linked with you. Besides, you haven't been shy about stating your antimarriage, anticommitment stance. Have you changed your mind about that?"

Digby scrubbed his hands over his face. Hell, no. But also, yes. Maybe a little. God, he didn't know…

Bay folded her arms across her chest, looking fiercely determined. "I'm going to court in two weeks to fight for custody. I can't take any chances. I *won't*."

If Bay were his mother, she'd say to hell with Olivia and take what she needed, what she wanted, putting her needs before her child's. But she wasn't Zia, she was Bay and loved her sister's child as her own. She was prepared to sacrifice anything and everything—including him—to do what was right. Digby felt annoyed, hurt and pissed off but he couldn't fault her for that.

A part of him even admired her commitment to her niece and to fulfilling her sister's wishes.

"I need us to go back to being what we were before today. Friends. Colleagues. Client and service provider."

He couldn't argue with her; he didn't have a leg to stand on. And he wouldn't, he had far more pride than that. And Bay was right, Olivia was all that was important.

Digby stepped back and slapped his hands on his hips. What else could he do but nod? "I get it," he growled.

Bay stroked his arm from elbow to shoulder. "I really don't think you do. You might not believe this, but I don't sleep around. Sleeping with you meant something to me, Digby, and I loved being with you. But the price I might pay if this gets out is too high. And I know that you understand that."

He wanted to argue with her, to persuade her that everything would be fine, that they could carry on, that no one would discover they were sleeping together. He was selfish enough to do that, ruthless and egotistical enough to put his needs before hers. And Liv's. He had, after all, learned from the best.

But he couldn't do that, not to Olivia and not to Bay. Neither of them deserved his selfishness and disrespect, and he wouldn't be able to live with himself. Olivia was not at fault and he wouldn't do anything to jeopardize her chances to stay with Bay.

Damn, putting other people first sucked. This was why he stayed single, why he didn't get involved.

"Once I get custody, we can rethink this," Bay quietly told him. "I just need two weeks, Dig."

But Digby knew that so much could happen in two weeks, in less time than that. Businesses could be lost, brothers could die, life could change in an instant. Nothing stayed the same, neither should it.

"I'm sorry our morning ended this way…"

Yeah, they should've just kept their mouths shut. Talking never did anyone any good. Bay lifted her shoulder up in a slight shrug and continued. "I'm going to get dressed and get going. Thanks for…" she gestured to the bed and her cheeks turned pink "…that."

Bay bit her bottom lip, shook her head and started to gather up her clothes. Quickly dressing, she shoved her feet into flip-flops and, after sending him another regretful look and quietly telling him that she'd see him on

Monday, walked out of his bedroom, leaving him standing there and feeling like a fool.

Not something he liked, or was used to feeling.

CHAPTER SEVEN

DIGBY STOOD TO the side of the grave, tears running down his face in a continuous stream. Above him, hard rain pounded on the roof of the white gazebo they'd erected over the grave to keep the matte black casket from floating to the top of the eight-foot pit.

Digby looked around, surprised to see Roisin standing behind him, and behind her Radd and Brin.

If Radd was here, then who was in the coffin?

Digby yelled for them to stop lowering the casket and sprang forward, desperate to see who he was burying.

His fingertips struggled to open the coffin.

His rough voice begged Radd to help him.

But Radd didn't step forward and he knew he was on his own.

Using all his strength, Digby lifted the

heavy lid, sensing that the casket was fighting him, that it wasn't happy to be opened.

With a final heave, Digby lifted the lid and allowed it to rest on its hinges. Taking a deep breath, still not wanting to look, he forced himself to open his eyes...

She looked peaceful.

The thought was coming from a place far, far away.

But everything that made her Bay was gone. Her vitality, the passion in those unusual eyes, her humor and her spirit. Her soul was gone and she'd taken his heart with her...

Digby was about to shut the lid of the casket when her eyes flew open and her hand reached out to grab his tie.

He stared down into her sad, sad eyes and waited for her to speak.

But instead of saying something profound, deeply meaningful, her eyes fluttered closed and Bay slipped away. And this time Digby knew she wasn't ever coming back...

His heart pounding, Digby shot up and looked around his bedroom, relieved to see the first rays of light peeking through the edges of the motorized blinds in his bedroom. Picking up the tablet from his bedside table, he tapped the button to open the blinds and as they rolled up he rubbed the sleep out of his eyes with his fingertips.

Damn, that had been a hell of a nightmare. Digby felt moisture on his fingertips and stared down at his hands, slowly registering that he'd been crying in his sleep.

Well, that was a first.

It was an overcast day, the mountain was concealed behind a thick cloud and the weather perfectly matched his mood. Sitting up, Digby rested his forearms on his knees, staring down at the damp print his palm left on his white sheet. He was, he decided, a basket case...

He'd had the same dream for most of his life but it was morphing into something deeper and darker, and every time he had the dream, he felt like he was losing a little bit of his soul. Maybe he should see someone...

And what would he say? *Hey, Doc, I've been having dreams about my brother dying most of my life. But this morning he was replaced by a woman I've only just recently met, whom I crave with every breath I take, with every beat of my heart. I want her; I need her. But I won't let myself have her. Because if I love her and she leaves me, that's me done. I'm not brave enough to take that risk...*

Loving someone and losing them? He refused to do it again.

Digby scrubbed his face with his hands, uncomfortable with the roiling, churning emotions swirling inside his gut.

A week had passed since Bay walked out of his bedroom and back into the friend zone and he was over it. Over the stilted conversations, over trying to keep his hands off her, over boycotting his office because it hurt too much to be around her and not be kissing her, laughing with her, goddamn talking to her.

Somehow, Bay Adair had snuck under his carefully constructed armor.

One week. In seven days, the custody hearing would be over—though he suspected Bay would want to wait a few weeks while the judge considered his decision—and then... what? What did he want from her, from this thing that was growing between them?

If he couldn't love Bay the way she needed to be loved, then he should let her go. But how could he? She was everything good and bright and colorful in his life.

She'd make his life better; the converse wasn't true.

Irritated with himself, Digby pushed the sheet back, thinking that he was damned if he did and damned if he didn't. He wanted Bay with an intensity that scared him but he'd never imagined himself settling down, making a solid commitment.

But neither could he imagine her not being in his life.

However, along with Bay came Olivia; that meant sharing Bay with Liv, and he wasn't ready for an instant family. That was one step too far. But, if they got to the point of dating, he and Olivia would start to develop a relationship, as well…

And if he ran true to form, and he always did, and decided that he wasn't cut out for attachment and permanence, Bay wouldn't be the only one who'd be hurt.

He didn't want to cause either of them any

pain. So he wouldn't. But that meant not being with Bay, ever again.

His stomach lurched into his throat.

Digby swung his legs over the edge of the bed and picked up his phone, looking for a distraction. As always, there were a slew of emails but one caught his eye. He read through it quickly, cursed, and immediately called Radd.

Radd, very unusually for him lately, answered his call.

"I take it you got the email then," Radd said, dispensing with their normal "how's business?" and "how's your holiday" small talk.

"Yeah."

"So, the beneficiary of our parents' trust is asking us to meet with them early next week."

Yeah, he got that; he'd read the damn email not five minutes ago. "Thank you, Captain Obvious," Digby muttered.

"Did you get out on the wrong side of the bed?" Radd asked him, sounding a trifle amused.

Digby told him what to do with himself and

immediately felt bad. It wasn't Radd's fault that he was horny and tired and frustrated. And confused. So damn confused.

"What's his motive?"

"You're assuming it's a man," Radd pointed out.

"His, her, *whatever*. Why does he want to meet us?" Digby demanded, standing up to pace his bedroom. He needed to work off some excess energy and when he was done with this call, he'd head for his lap pool and push his body until he banished Bay's lovely face from the big screen in his head.

"I guess we'll find out next week," Radd laconically replied.

"On one hand, I don't care about the money or collections of cars, art and property—we both have enough to carry us through several lifetimes. But I am curious as to who Gil and Zia thought important enough to warrant such generosity."

"Me too," Radd admitted. "Once we know, we can put the parents behind us."

He'd like nothing better than to put his parents, their deaths, his past with them and the mystery surrounding their inheritance to bed, forever. He had more important things to worry about.

Like Bay...

Annoyed with himself for allowing his thoughts to return to her—not that they were ever really off her—Digby told Radd he was looking forward to seeing him, and to him getting back to work, and disconnected.

Digby tapped the face of his phone against his forehead and hoped that the day would be kind to him. Honestly, at this point, he didn't know if he needed a liter of coffee, six shots of tequila or to sleep for a month. Or all three.

Or Bay.

Mostly, he reluctantly admitted, he just needed Bay, any way he could get her.

Later that day and on the other side of the property, Bay sat on the Persian carpet in Digby's office, surrounded by fabric swatches and wallpaper samples. She'd yet to find the exact fabric and wallpaper combination she wanted for the ballroom.

She was not usually this indecisive and it was driving her nuts. Maybe she needed to take the sample books up to the ballroom and look at them in the natural light, but she'd tried that already and the entire exercise just made her feel more confused.

And self-doubt was creeping in...

She'd told Digby she couldn't do this. What made her, or him, think that she could take on a project this size? It was nuts; she had no experience, no track record. This fabric cost thousands of dollars a yard, what if she made a mistake?

Bay leaned forward and banged her forehead on the book in front of her, feeling her back muscles stretching as she did the once-familiar movement. She hadn't done any yoga or Pilates for months; she was risking tearing a muscle thinking she was as flexible as she was earlier in the year.

What she wouldn't do for a hot-stone, full-body massage...

Digby had told her, a while ago, that she could use the hotel's spa at no cost, but it wasn't something she felt comfortable doing, especially since they were...well, not at odds, but their relationship had shifted.

Since sleeping together, they were both behaving like polite strangers, both pretending that they hadn't been intimate, physically as well as mentally. These days their meetings and interactions were both brief and rushed, mostly because Digby was rarely around.

Bay wasn't a fool; she knew that Digby was spending more time at Tempest-Vane headquarters to avoid her.

But she missed him, she missed who they were together.

Bay sat up slowly, picked up her water bottle and took a long sip. Leaning back on her hands, she stared at the art on Digby's walls, seascapes that never failed to soothe her. Except today, today she was fairly certain that not even a strong hit of Valium would do the trick.

She was tired, she hadn't slept well in weeks, her creativity had all but dried up and Olivia, obviously picking up on her stress, was being a monster and fighting her on anything and everything.

Thank God for Roisin.

Thank God, and all his angels, archangels, saints and deities, for Roisin.

Feeling like the walls were closing in on her, Bay stood up and walked out of Digby's office and down the staff corridor. Thinking that she'd take a walk in The Vane's impressive gardens, she slipped into the lobby and ducked around three businessmen waiting for a lift.

The lobby was full of guests and Bay wrinkled her nose as clashing perfumes and the scent of the huge floral bouquets drifted over her. Heading left, she crossed the lovely harlequin floor, aiming for the wide French doors that led to the wraparound veranda.

The back of her neck tingled and Bay recognized that sensation; it meant that Digby was near. Looking around, she saw him standing by the concierge's desk, talking to a small group who'd obviously just arrived.

Italian, Bay decided. Florence or Milan. Big money, judging by the Birkin bags, the Louboutin shoes and the huge diamonds on fingers and earlobes.

One woman had her hand on Digby's forearm, and he was laughing. The man added something and Digby clapped him on his back, before turning to the waiter standing behind him holding a tray of glasses filled with what she knew to be a superb vintage of Moët & Chandon.

Digby handed out glasses, flashing his broad, sexy grin.

He loved this, Bay realized. He loved interacting with his guests, playing the part of the genial host. Some of it was based in his need for attention but a good portion of it was his genuine love for people, for making them feel welcome, happy and looked after.

All the things he'd never experienced growing up within his own family. Neither, she admitted, had she.

Bay stopped by a column, concealed by a huge bouquet of mixed flowers, and watched as another two men approached Digby, who was standing to the side of the group. Digby caught their eye, held up a discreet finger asking them to wait and, with ease, disengaged himself from the Italians. The men waiting for him shook his hand and Bay saw the genuine pleasure on their faces.

People liked Digby, she realized. They liked him a lot.

He was extraordinarily self-confident and bold and in being so unapologetic about it, he silently encouraged people to follow his lead. People felt more alive around him; she certainly did. Just knowing him promised some sort of adventure, and people were attracted to individuals who could make their lives more interesting.

Bay was.

Ah, hell. Attracted to him? She was more than halfway in love with him. What a stupid thing to have done, Bay thought. She could just, well, kick herself.

Bay held her hand up to her face to hide her yawn and slowly made her way across the floor, hoping a brisk walk would raise her flagging energy levels and, hopefully, spark her creativity. And clear her head...

Bay felt her phone vibrate and she pulled it out of the pocket of her cotton pants. Swiping her thumb across the screen, her heart—stupid, stupid thing—leaped when she saw Digby's name on the screen.

My office. Now.

Frowning at his unusually autocratic text message, Bay looked around, didn't see Digby and retraced her steps back toward his office.

After punching in the code that gave her access to the back rooms of the hotel, she pulled open the door and walked down the passage. Stepping into Monica's office, she started to greet Digby's assistant and realized that she wasn't there. Hearing the door shut behind her, she whirled around and slammed into Digby's hard chest. She clocked the sound of the outer door locking but before she could make sense of what was happening, Digby's mouth was on hers and she spun away on a vortex of pleasure.

She allowed herself a minute to indulge in the wonderful feel and taste of him before pulling back and putting some distance between them, her breathing so labored she felt like she'd run a fast five miles' race.

"I saw you walking across the lobby and realized that I couldn't go one more day, one more goddamn minute, without touching you."

Bay looked into his eyes, midnight blue and a little feral, a lot wild. Needing to connect with him, just a little, she placed her hand on his chest, feeling his thundering heartbeat. Hers was pumping at maximum capacity, as well. God, she'd missed him. Working near him and not being able to touch him had tested her willpower every minute of every day.

She was thrilled that Digby was suffering, as well.

But, as powerful and as feminine as that made her feel—having a man like Digby looking at her like she was everything he wanted and needed was a high she'd never experienced before—she *had* to be sensible and cautious.

"We can't do this, Digby. I told you that."

"One kiss, Bay. I've missed your mouth."

She'd missed him too, dreadfully. And what would one kiss hurt? There were no cameras in Digby's private offices; nobody would know. She needed this quick interlude to slake a little of the desire that raged through her.

Digby's mouth connected with hers and Bay felt that hit of lightning, that spike of need. Yeah, this. This man, this moment…

When Digby moved his hands up to hold her face in his, tilting her head to take their kiss deeper and darker, Bay stroked his waist from hip to rib cage.

"I think about you all the time and not being able to touch you is so damn hard," Digby muttered as he dropped sexy kisses on her jaw, across her cheekbone. "I'm so damn hard. All the time."

As if to prove his point, Digby pushed his erection into her stomach and Bay released a tortured moan. She wanted him, in her hands, in her mouth…everywhere. She'd never felt so out of control and she loved it.

She loved kissing this wild man, charming and complicated.

His mouth came back to hers and his tongue found hers, stroking it. His taste was delicious, his breath sweet. And with every thrust, each parry, she could feel herself losing control. She wanted him, no, worse, she *needed* him.

And because that need was so fierce, so crazy intense, Bay knew she had to back away before he overwhelmed her senses and desire shut down her ability to think rationally. Her body was betraying her; her willpower had gone AWOL. And because she couldn't afford to lose herself in him, she yanked herself out of Digby's arms and moved back until she was out of arm's reach.

In his eyes, she saw lust and regret and frustration. Stepping back, he raked the fingers of both hands through his hair.

"We can't do this," Bay whispered.

"I know," Digby replied, his voice sounding strangled. He pulled in a deep breath, rubbed his hands over his face and tipped his head back to look at the ceiling. After a minute he spoke again. "Monica will be back in five minutes."

Bay nodded and watched as Digby, before her eyes, transformed from her wild, intense lover into the debonair, suave businessman he always was. While she knew her cheeks were still burning, her nipples were throbbing and her intimate area was screaming for him to touch her, he looked like he'd just come from a business meeting.

Even his pants had subsided. He was in control and she wasn't. The realization that she was the one who could lose everything—Olivia and her heart—yet he'd lose nothing, smacked her in the gut.

Bay placed her hands flat on Monica's desk and blinked back unshed tears. She would be, she knew, easily replaceable in his life—

sex was easy to find and this was the guy who didn't do commitment or forever, remember?—but Bay doubted he'd ever be replaced in hers.

Sure, he wasn't the only guy in the universe...

But he was the only one who mattered.

Hearing Digby's low curse, she sighed when he placed his hands on her waist and gently turned her around. His eyes drifted across her face and he lifted a thumb to graze its pad over the soft skin under her eyes. "Goddammit, Bay, you're exhausted."

Bay looked into his red-rimmed eyes and raised one eyebrow. "Kettle. Pot. Black."

Digby acknowledged her verbal hit with a quick half smile. Hearing the office door open, he stepped away from her, his eyes not leaving her face. "And that has to change," he said, ignoring Monica as she pushed past them to settle in behind her desk.

Digby took Bay's wrist and pulled her into the passage, away from Monica's flapping ears. He slid his hands into the pockets of his suit pants, his expression intense.

"Do you trust me, Bay?"

What a strange, out-of-the-blue question. Behind her back, Bay placed her palms against the cool wall and considered how to answer him. She did trust him, with her body and her feelings, but not with her heart. Never with her heart.

Digby spoke again before she could answer. "If I solemnly swear to respect your privacy issue and that not a word of us being together will reach the press, will you come away with me, for a few days?"

She'd love nothing more but she had Olivia to think of. "I can't be separated from Liv, Digby, not right now. I need to be with her, especially if the custody hearing doesn't go my way."

"It will go your way, and I understand that," Digby said, darting a look down the still empty hallway. "My invitation includes Liv—I get that you two are a package deal.

"Besides," he added, "Olivia is my favorite three-year-old."

"She's the only three-year-old you know," Bay pointed out, amused and touched at his easy acceptance of Olivia.

"Fair point but I still like her. With regard to going away, I'll see what I can organize," Digby said and winced at Monica bellowing his name.

Bay watched him walk back into his office and shook her head. Going away sounded like a lovely idea but she knew how busy Digby was, how inundated they both were. When he hit his desk and work rolled over him, he'd realize how ambitious the thought was and that leaving for the weekend really wasn't an option.

The thought counted, Bay thought, touched that Digby was worried about her. It was a lovely idea but it wasn't practical so Bay pushed it from her mind.

The next day, Digby had just finished making a series of calls to put his plan into action when he heard a quick rap on his office door, quickly followed by Olivia's high-pitched squeal. He lifted his head and there she was, barreling across the room to him, her smile powerful enough to compete with the sun.

"Dig, I was looks for you."

Digby caught her, swung her up onto his lap and lifted an eyebrow in Roisin's direction. The nanny shrugged and rolled her eyes. "She got this bee in her bonnet and I've heard nothing but your name all morning. I asked around, heard you were in here and thought you could give her a little attention."

"And you a break," Digby dryly replied, and Roisin flashed an unrepentant smile. Roisin was his employee but didn't act like it. "I'm glad you are here—I was about to call you."

Roisin frowned. "Problem?"

Digby quickly shook his head. "You have the weekend off. I'm whipping these two away for a long weekend."

Roisin smiled. "Nice. Where to?"

Digby reached around Olivia's little body to minimize his computer screen. "I wanted to go to our safari operation, Kagiso—I thought someone would get a kick out of seeing an elephant. But it's fully booked and my villa is being used by a friend this long weekend."

"I wants an elephant," Olivia told him, proof that she was definitely listening to their conversation. "He can sleep in my bed and I'll call him Fluffy."

"The penguin she wanted last week was also called Fluffy," Roisin told him, sotto voce.

"I'm taking them to a luxurious beach resort in Mozambique," Digby told Roisin. He'd thought long and hard on where to go, looking for a place that was both isolated and interesting, finally remembering that the Tempest-Vane Holdings leisure division was considering buying a five-star resort in Mozambique on one of the small islands in the Bazaruto Archipelago. He and Radd had been meaning to make a trip up there but hadn't gotten that far...

Five minutes later, he had a number in his hand and ten minutes later, he had the excited owner promising him their best villa. He'd fly the Tempest-Vane helicopter to the airport, hop on their private jet and in a few hours the three of them could be sitting on the beach as the sun went down.

"I'm worried about her. She's tired and stressed," Digby told Roisin, remembering her blue-ringed eyes and gaunt face.

Roisin looked worried. "I know. She came to see Olivia earlier and I could tell she'd been crying." Roisin tucked a long dark curl behind her ear. "If you take her away, you can't let her work—she has to eat decent food and you have to make sure she relaxes and sleeps. She needs to be at her best next week."

"Yes, mom," Digby dryly responded. Roisin was acting like a mother hen. Then again, he was acting like one too.

Wait, she'd mentioned next week…

"So you know about the custody hearing?" Digby asked. If so, she and Roisin were closer than he'd realized.

"I do. And I made a witness statement saying what a great mom she is," Roisin replied. Digby saw the concern in her eyes. "But how are you going to make sure that nobody knows she's with you, Digby? She's terrified of the press linking the two of you together."

He was aware. While he knew it was necessary, it still pissed him off.

"I've snuck in many a high-profile guest for a press-free, low-key weekend at The Vane. I'm sure I can use those same skills to smuggle them off the premises without anyone knowing. Helicopters and private planes ensure privacy."

"And what about clothes and toiletries?" Roisin asked.

"I put in a call to the manager of the boutique on the premises and if she needs to, she'll employ the services of a personal shopper to get everything they need."

Roisin, finally, looked impressed. "You've thought of everything."

He hoped so. Now he just had to get Bay and Liv to the helipad at the back of the property. Digby, impatient to leave, turned back to the screen. His eyes fell to Olivia's hands and he muttered a quiet curse when he saw she was drawing squiggles on his tie. How the hell had she managed to do that without either of them noticing?

Digby saw that Roisin was about to chastise Olivia but he lifted his hand to wave her off. "It's just a tie."

"It's a damn expensive tie."

Pale green and ever so slightly embossed with a fine gray pattern, it was Hermès and a limited edition. But still, just a tie.

Digby stood up and placed Olivia, who was still holding his ink-covered tie in her hand, on his hip. Roisin held out her arms to Liv and Digby transferred his sweet-smelling bundle to her. "Let's go, princess, we've got stuff to do."

Olivia pursed her rosebud mouth. "'Kay. Are we going to see Mommy Bay? 'Cos I want to ask her if I can have an elephant."

Digby grinned and dropped a kiss on her nose. "You do that, kid. Maybe she'll be more reasonable than Ro-Ro."

"Funny," Roisin said, as she left his office.

Again, no deference. And, again, he really didn't mind.

CHAPTER EIGHT

OLIVIA LOVED THE helicopter ride to the airport, Bay not so much. It wasn't that she didn't like flying and, while she was fully confident of Digby's ability to handle the craft—like everything else he did, he operated the helicopter with complete control and confidence—she just wasn't crazy about the amount of space between her and the ground.

But the combination of a helicopter and private jet flying meant a quick trip to Bazaruto Island. They'd arrived way before sunset and had been able to take Olivia to the beach and to explore the rock pools directly below the house. There were, Bay thought, perks to being megarich.

She'd never been to Mozambique before and she was very happy to have been kidnapped and whisked away to this aqua playground with her two favorite people. The Bazaruto Archipelago was, as Radd had told her, a protected marine reserve and national park, a place where the sand dunes rolled onto the white sand beaches playing kiss-kiss with the clear, azure ocean.

It was all that and more. Stunningly beautiful and indescribably romantic.

The villa was also amazing. It was a modern, super luxurious open-plan building with four bedrooms, as many bathrooms and a huge living area with one-eighty-degree views of the sea and sand. The shaded entertainment area, dotted with comfortable loungers, overlooked the rock pools. It was a minute walk through the dune grass to a private beach. The next house, Digby told her, was a distance away; they were completely and utterly secluded.

Bay pulled a sheet up Olivia's tiny body and pushed her curls off her forehead. She'd run herself ragged on the beach, and bathing and feeding the exhausted toddler had been a nightmare. But Bay managed both and, not two minutes after her head was on the pillow, she was deeply asleep.

Bay straightened and walked to the window of this room she'd chosen for Olivia to sleep in, looking at the dark sea and the rising moon. When she had arrived at the helipad, situated at the back of The Vane's property, and listened to Digby's plan for a weekend away, her first instinct was to refuse. Then he told her that it came with no strings, that they'd both been working like demons and they all deserved a weekend away. They both needed, he insisted, to relax.

She just had to step into the helicopter; everything else had been taken care of. Nobody would know they were together. It was a break from reality and God she needed it.

And now that she was here, and after swimming in the lukewarm ocean and watching a magnificent sunset, she was glad she hadn't refused. Digby was right; she needed this...

Needed peace and quiet. But mostly she simply needed to be with Digby.

Bay dropped a kiss on Olivia's head and left her sleeping, leaving the door ajar in case she woke up and called for her. Heading back into the open-plan living area, she looked around for Digby and saw that he'd jumped into the pool situated in the corner of the deck. Bay watched as he broke through the surface of the water to rest his forearms on the paving, his chin on his wrist as he looked out to sea.

Seeing a bottle of wine and two glasses sitting on the wooden table, she poured the wine, picked up both glasses and walked over to the pool. Sinking to the pavement, she handed Digby a glass and dropped her bare calf and foot into the water.

Digby looked at her and smiled. "I like this place."

Bay sighed, tipping her head back to look at the stars popping through the black velvet sky. "It's fabulous."

"Do you think we should buy it?" Digby casually asked. "It's up for sale."

Bay nearly choked on her wine when he told her the selling price.

Holy cupcakes, that was a hell of a lot of money.

"Ah, maybe you should see the rest of the property before you make a decision," Bay suggested, her tone wry.

Digby picked up her foot, kissed the arch of her instep before dropping her foot back into the water. "Good point."

Bay rested the cool wineglass against her

cheek. "Thank you for bringing me here, Digby. For bringing both of us. I...well... I needed this."

Digby's eyes and the darkening sea were both the same intense shade of blue. He stared at her for a long moment before nodding. "I know."

Bay watched as he propelled himself out of the pool, arm muscles bulging as he left the water. He walked over to the lounger, picked up a towel and started drying his body. Wrapping his towel over his wet swimming shorts, he walked back over to her, holding out his hand. Bay placed her hand in his and he hauled her up, keeping hold of her as she found her feet. Because she wanted to, Bay placed her hand on his chest, her thumb brushing water off it.

"I missed you," Bay said, the words slipping out without her permission.

Digby placed his lips on her temple and his big hands on her hips. "I missed you too."

Bay slid her arms around his waist and rested her cheek on his wet chest and listened to his strong heartbeat. His arms encircled her, hauled her closer and it felt like he was putting himself between her and the world. She was a strong, independent woman but sometimes it felt so wonderful to lean, to soak in someone else's strength.

And Digby had a lot of it, mental and physical.

Digby's hands left her body to hold her face, his thumbs on her cheekbones and then her jaw. "This place is utterly secluded, Bay, so we can pretend that there's just the two of us—"

"Three," Bay reminded him.

"Two and a half." Digby's lips twitched into a smile. He rubbed his thumb across her bottom lip. "I have a lot on my mind, so do you, so the aim of this weekend is not to think but just to be. Think we can do that?"

God, that idea sounded like heaven. She needed a break from thinking about the fight for custody of Liv. She couldn't stop the thought that losing Liv would be like losing Layla all over again and, as a result, her stomach was twisted in a perpetual knot.

Bay rubbed the back of her neck. She wanted to stop thinking, to take a break from missing Digby and worrying about the future.

She desperately wanted to live in the moment, this moment, and Digby was offering her the opportunity to do just that.

Digby tipped her head up with a finger under her chin. "Is that a deal?"

Bay nodded. "Absolutely. Can I just ask you one thing?"

Apprehension jumped into Digby's eyes and she felt bad for putting it there. "Sure," he replied, sounding a little wary.

Bay hesitated before deciding to take the plunge. If this was the only time she'd have with him then she wasn't going to waste it. "Will you kiss me? Like you did before?"

Passion flared in Digby's eyes. "I have no problem with that request..." He started to lower his mouth to hers but Bay stepped back and held out her hand.

"One more thing?"

Impatience warred with desire as both emotions danced across his face. "Getting impatient here, Adair," Digby muttered.

She loved the fact that she could make him growl. Not being very experienced in dirty talk or in the art of seduction, she looked for words to turn him on. Though, judging by his tented towel, he was already halfway there. "I'd like to spend the weekend in your arms, in your bed."

"Excellent news," Digby muttered.

She could tell him; she was sure he'd understand. He knew that Olivia and her happiness and stability were her driving force. "It's just that, when we are back in Cape Town, I can't—"

Digby placed his broad hand over her mouth and shook his head. "No, sweetheart. No explanations, not now. I just want to love you."

Oh, thank God. Wonderful.

"Right now, I think it's time the kissing began," Digby murmured, pulling her against his body. He started at the corner of her mouth and Bay felt the tilt of his lips as he smiled. Tension and stress swirled away as his hands ran over her shoulders, down her arms, up her sides. Holding her rib cage with both hands, he spread his fingers and his thumbs brushed her nipples. They immediately flowered under his attention. Her tongue met his in a long, lust-soaked tangle and Bay noticed that he went from hard to concrete in a nanosecond. She was back, in his arms, in his life, for this weekend.

It felt more than right.

It felt like perfection.

Bay ran her hands up Digby's back, over his butt, across his stomach. Her fingers danced over his six-pack and hit the band of his towel. Unhooking the edges, she allowed it to fall to the deck. That was the first barrier; the second was the ties of his board shorts. Undoing the knot, she loosened the ties and pushed the fabric down his hips and past his knees and then dropped the shorts to the deck. Her hand unerringly found him, encircled him, her thumb sweeping across the tip while her mouth supplied him with emotion-soaked kisses.

"Let's get your clothes off, sweet Bay."

While it would be wonderful to make love outside, she still had to consider Olivia waking up and needing her. "Can we take this somewhere a little more private?" Bay asked him. "We have a child in the house."

It took a moment for Digby to remember Olivia and when he did, he nodded. Taking Bay's hand again, he picked up his towel and shorts and, walking naked across the deck, led her to the end of it. They turned the corner and stepped onto a semiprivate deck. Two more loungers lay outside what she knew to be the master bedroom, and Digby sat down on a lounger and guided her to sit on his bare thighs. She was still dressed in her T-shirt and shorts and she wanted him to rip the clothes from her body, feeling like they were slowly constricting her.

She wanted to be naked. *Now.*

"Digby," she pleaded as he dropped kisses on her jawline.

"Mmm...?"

"I've got far too many clothes on and I need your hands on me."

"Do you?" Digby smiled as he toyed with the hem of her T-shirt. "You sound a bit impatient, darling."

"You have no idea," Bay grumbled, holding his chin and jaw with one hand before covering his mouth with hers. She sighed when he allowed her tongue to slide in, to explore his masculine mouth. She'd missed him; she'd missed this so much. Making love to Digby made her feel powerful, like a pagan woman, put on this earth to pursue pleasure.

Loving Digby made the world stop, problems fade.

But kissing Digby and only having his hands resting on her waist wasn't doing it for her. She needed him wild and passionate and out of control.

"Digby, if you don't start touching me, I'm going to lose it," Bay warned him, after pulling her mouth off his.

"We can't have that now, can we?" He lifted her to sit closer to his knees and spread her legs wider. Bay gasped as Digby slid his hands up her inner thighs, under the loose cotton of her shorts, his knuckles flirting with her feminine, intimate area. He rubbed and teased but it wasn't enough; she wanted more. She wanted everything he could give her.

"Digby!"

"Patience, my darling Bay. Teasing you is half the fun."

Bay sucked in her breath when his index finger pushed under the material of her thong and slid into her moist channel. Her head tipped back. "Digby, ah. Jeez, that feels good."

"Take off your bra and shirt, sweetheart."

Bay whipped her T-shirt off, flicked open the clasp to her bra and tossed the garments away. Then Digby's hot mouth was on her nipple and a bolt of heat, sensation and pure power flashed through her system, and Bay found herself teetering on the edge of a powerful wave, waiting to fly down its massive face.

Digby held her eyes as his second finger joined the first and he brushed her bundle of nerves with his thumb. "Do I make you feel good, Bay?"

"You make me feel amazing, Dig," Bay replied from a place far, far away. She was standing on that wave, waiting. Another second and she'd be flying.

"So close, Dig," she said, placing her arms behind her head and gripping hair in her fingers, trying to hold on, trying to delay her flight.

Digby rocked his fingers within her, hitting a spot deeper inside, and Bay shouted as she accelerated, skating down that warm, rolling wave with all the skill of a world champion. She felt Digby's face in her neck, his fingers digging into her hip, but she didn't care. She didn't want this intense ride, the sexual equivalent of riding one of the ocean's big waves, to end.

After sucking every last sensation out of the most intense orgasm of her life, Bay collapsed against Digby's chest, yawned and snuggled in. Like Olivia, she was exhausted, and there was nothing like fresh air, sex and the sea to lull one into sleep.

Digby stood up with her in his arms and walked into the master bedroom. He lowered her to the bed and draped a lightweight cotton blanket over her. "Sleep for a little while, Bay. I'll wake you when dinner is ready."

Bay yawned and forced her eyes open. They immediately drooped closed again. She waved in what she hoped was the direction of his groin. She had but he hadn't... "What about, you know...you?"

"I'm good." Digby dropped a kiss on her forehead. "Hopefully, we can pick that up later. But for now, sleep."

Bay yawned again and, wrapping her arms around a pillow, wishing it were Digby, dropped off to sleep.

Bay woke ninety minutes later and, after a quick shower and changing into a short sleeveless dress, checked on Olivia. She'd kicked her blankets off and spread out; Bay knew that she'd sleep through, hopefully allowing her to sleep in, as well.

Pushing her hand through her hair, Bay walked into the kitchen and inhaled the distinctive and wonderful smell of fried onions and beef burgers. Following her nose, she returned to the entertainment deck to see Digby standing by the monstrous gas grill, wearing a bright pink apron with the words Kiss the Cook on the bib.

Since that was an order she was happy to obey, Bay placed her hand on his chest and did what she was told. Digby tasted her briefly before pulling back. He sent her an easy grin. "If we start that we won't get food and I'm starving."

So was she. Bay dropped into a chair, crossed her legs and nodded when Digby offered her a beer. Eschewing a glass, she took the icy Mexican brew he offered, complete with a slice of lime, and took a long sip. "What's the time?" she idly asked.

Digby consulted his bells-and-whistles-and-the-kitchen-sink watch. "A little more than half past eight."

The sun set earlier here than it did in Cape Town and it was now fully dark. Digby had flicked on the lights to the house and entertainment area and Bay imagined that ships at sea could see straight into the house. Thank God there weren't any other houses for miles around.

"I was looking through your portfolio of drawings for the hotel while you were sleeping," Digby said, picking up his own bottle of beer and taking a sip.

Bay wrinkled her nose. "I am not happy with what I've come up with for the new honeymoon suite. It's blah…"

"I think you are being too hard on yourself—I thought it was great."

It really wasn't, but she appreciated his comment. "I'm missing something. Hopefully it'll come to me sooner rather than later."

Digby lifted the lid of the gas barbecue to check on the beef patties. "You went to Stellies, right?"

Bay nodded, smiling at his use of the nickname for her old university, the University of Stellenbosch.

"I didn't know you could do a degree in interior design there."

Bay rested her head against the back of the chair. "I didn't do a degree in interior design—I did a diploma after I graduated."

Digby looked confused. "Then what did you get a degree in?"

"Mechanical engineering."

Digby lowered his beer bottle to stare at her. "Seriously?"

Bay nodded. "As a heart attack. I hated every bloody minute of it, but yeah, I got it done. I'm even still registered with the engineering council."

Digby placed his beer down and his hands on the table, staring at her. "Wait, hold on, let me get this straight. You have a degree in mechanical engineering?"

"Yep."

"And you hated it?"

"Yep."

"So why didn't you change courses? Do something else?" Digby demanded, standing up again.

Ah, that. Bay winced, took a sip of her beer and rested her bare feet on the seat of the chair opposite her. After helping herself to a juicy black olive from the bowl next to her, she popped it into her mouth and slowly chewed. Damn, they tasted good, like the ones she had on Lesbos two years ago.

"The short answer to that is that I didn't change courses because I'm damn stubborn, especially when it comes to anything to do with my parents."

"What's the long answer?"

Bay picked the paper label from her bottle. "My dad's first choice for his three daughters was for them to leave school and marry. That's what good girls did, what my oldest sister, Jane, did. And if they did want to get a qualification, then becoming a nurse, teacher or secretary was acceptable...just."

"Does he know it's the twenty-first century?" Digby demanded.

Bay smiled. "Anyway, what my dad didn't

bank on was that his two younger daughters would inherit his brains."

Bay wrinkled her nose. "Not meaning to brag but school was easy for me, as it was for Layla. I got a full academic scholarship to Foresters and so did Layla, a year later.

"I skipped a year of school and graduated early. My father wanted me to teach—I thought I'd rather put my head in an oven. In a fit of pique, I decided to show him I could do what he does, so I applied to join the Faculty of Engineering. I was admitted and I thought he'd blow a gasket. What did women know about engineering? I wasn't suited, I would drop out, I was wasting my time…"

"But you stuck it out."

"Never been so bored in my life." She didn't bother to tell him that she'd graduated third in her class and briefly considered doing her MBA. "He was ridiculously angry that the firm he worked for offered for me to join the company when I finished my postgrad degree."

"I bet."

Digby whipped the burgers off the grill

onto a plate and swiftly started to assemble them from the ingredients he'd prepared earlier. Lettuce, tomato, pickles, fried onions, what looked like spicy mayonnaise.

She placed a hand on her stomach, realizing how hungry she was.

"As soon as I graduated, I immediately enrolled in a course to do a diploma in interior design. When I got that, I rewarded myself with a holiday in Thailand. Then I went to Vietnam, then to Cambodia and basically, I kept traveling for six years. I was so damn happy to be away from Cape Town, from everyone but Layla.

"At some point during my travels, I realized I was wasting my energy on my father and that my anger was destroying me, not him. It was just so damn hard to stop being angry at him." Bay stared out to sea, her thoughts a million miles away. "I saw him, you know. A day or two before I first met you."

Digby frowned. "Really? What did he want?"

"He told me that he wanted Liv, that I would be forgiven if I just handed her over. That I

230 HOW TO WIN THE WILD BILLIONAIRE

could be part of the family again if I agreed." Bay rubbed her fingertips across her forehead. "I was, sort of, tempted. I could give them Liv, I could go back to traveling and I'd have my family back…"

Bay darted a look in Digby's direction but there was no judgment on his face. "So, why didn't you?" he asked, his voice remaining even.

"Because I knew that he was using Liv to manipulate me, to get me to, finally, fall into line. My father doesn't like being bested, especially by a woman."

"How did you beat him, Bay?"

Bay picked a slice of gherkin and slowly chewed it as she pondered his question. "That's difficult to explain. By being as stubborn as him, I guess."

She hesitated before continuing. "I've told you that he was racist and misogynistic and I hated his views, but it went deeper than that. I mean, I loathed the fact that he had such antiquated views and we had screaming arguments about his inability to consider another point of view. But what really hurt me terribly was that he couldn't love me if I didn't have the same opinion as him."

"What do you mean?" Digby asked, pushing a plated burger over to her.

"Before I left for Foresters, I was his favorite girl. I adored him and he adored me too. We spent so much time together—I loved being with him. And when he's not being a jerk, he can be engaging and rather wonderful."

Digby picked up his burger, took a bite, his eyes and all his attention on her.

"But after I started challenging him, he withdrew. We had a dozen vicious arguments and hundreds of minor ones but instead of trying to understand, he punished me by distancing himself from me."

"I'm so sorry, baby," Digby murmured.

Bay folded her arms across her chest, her need for food gone. She stared at the dark sea, listening to the waves crashing. Thinking about her parents and the upcoming custody battle made her throat close and her lungs feel like they were being squeezed in a vise.

She couldn't lose Liv, she couldn't...

Bay heard Digby's muffled curse and then

he was on his haunches in front of her, his hands on her thighs, pulling her back to the here and now. Needing to stabilize herself, she lifted her fingers to touch his cheek.

Digby moved his head to kiss her fingers. "Let's make a deal, sweetheart?"

"Mmm? What's that?"

"For the next few days, it's just us. We're not going to think about work or deals or useless parents and custody battles or my meeting with whoever my parents left their money to—"

Bay's mouth dropped open. "You're meeting them? Who is it? Do you know?"

Digby grimaced. "No idea. Radd and I will meet with him next week. The meeting will be at the same time as your custody hearing on Tuesday."

Right. Well, Tuesday was going to be a big day for them both.

Digby ran his hands up the outside of her thighs and Bay, as she always did, wanted more. "Let's take this time, sweetheart, just for us and not let the outside world intrude. Can we do that?"

Bay slowly nodded. That sounded like heaven.

For the next few days, she was going to live for the moment, enjoy her time with Digby and face whatever came her way next week. Digby squeezed her legs and stood up.

"Excellent. So, do me a favor and eat your burger because you're going to need the energy tonight."

Now there was an incentive she could get behind. Smiling at the thought, she pulled her plate toward her and sliced her burger in two. Then she picked up one half and bit down, groaning with delight.

Digby grinned at her and wiped his mouth with a paper napkin. "Good?"

"Better than sex," Bay replied, her mouth full of food.

"Oh, it bloody well isn't and I intend to prove that to you."

Bay laughed and waved her burger in the air. "Can I finish my food first?"

Digby tapped his watch. "You have fifteen minutes, Adair."

Ten minutes later, shortly after she swallowed her last bite, Digby picked her up, tossed her over his shoulder and walked her to his bedroom.

And, as he promised, the sex was better than the burger.

Digby felt the sun on his face and adjusted his cap to keep it out of his eyes. This was turning out to be a perfect day. The sun was hot but not blistering and the sea was refreshingly cool. Earlier this morning, he'd left Bay asleep in his bed and hit the beach as dawn broke. After a long run, he'd swum out to beyond the reef and back, feeling the burn in his legs and arms. When he finally returned to the house, he rinsed off in the outdoor shower, checked whether Olivia was still asleep and climbed back into bed with Bay, waking her up with a series of X-rated kisses.

After they made love for the second time, Bay made coffee, and he'd been drifting back to sleep when a three-foot dynamo jumped on his stomach, demanding to go to the beach. She hadn't been prepared to hear the word *no*.

He'd swum with Olivia, watched as Bay made sand castles with her, and he had rubbed sun cream over Bay's skin, sneaking in a kiss whenever he was sure Olivia's attention was otherwise occupied.

Making love to Bay was wonderful, Digby decided, but spending out-of-bed time with her was as much fun. He enjoyed Olivia, loved her cheeky conversation and her piping voice and her enthusiasm for, well, *everything*.

"How are you feeling about meeting the heir to your parents' estate next week?" Bay asked him, out of the blue.

Digby lifted his cap to look at her but she was staring out to sea. After admiring her profile for a while, he closed his eyes again and readjusted his cap.

"I don't really care one way or the other."

Bay poked him in the ribs with her index finger. "That's a cop-out, Dig—you have to feel something about the person."

She wasn't going to let this go. "Okay, I'm annoyed that some random person is going to enjoy the benefits of a century-plus of my ancestors' hard work. And they'd better not think that this tenuous connection will create a bond between him and Radd and I. I have no intention of playing happy families. Radd is all the family I need."

"Because you are a lone wolf, right?" Bay asked, her voice soft.

Yeah, exactly that. But lately, he'd started to think that he might, one day, be able to do this family thing.

Maybe.

And maybe, possibly, he might; at some point in the future, he'd even want this enough to risk having his heart mangled if it—love and a family—disappeared on him.

And maybe Bay was the one person, the only person, who could make him feel this way. She was the first woman to have him contemplating permanence and commitment. He liked her, he liked her more than any woman he'd ever met before. He adored her body, and sex was, well, a revelation. Instead of it being a nice, satisfactory, albeit a bit of a mechanical act, making love with Bay was a feast of textures and tastes and sensations and sounds. Instead of pulling back after achievement of sexual satisfaction and creating physical, and emotional, distance, Digby normally stayed where he was, wanting to hold on to the moment as long as possible. Gentle kisses were exchanged, backs were rubbed, hands caressed.

For the first time ever, he felt emotionally connected to a woman and for once, he didn't feel like running for the hills. Whatever was happening between him and Bay felt right and he was going to enjoy it for as long as it lasted. And God, although he knew that nothing lasted forever—that it *couldn't*—he hoped Bay would be in his life for the longest time.

Bay *and* Olivia. Because they were a package deal.

"You had a nightmare last night," Bay softly said, jerking him out of his rambling musings. Forcing himself not to react, Digby stayed where he was, conscious of his suddenly thundering heart. He didn't remember any dreams from last night but obviously something had happened for Bay to reach that conclusion.

Before he could ask, Bay carried on speaking. "You were horribly agitated—at some point I actually thought you might be crying."

Crap. Digby winced. *How bloody embarrassing.*

"What were you dreaming about, Dig?"

He could brush her off, tell her that it was nothing, that he didn't remember. But they were long past white lies and inanities, and to hand her either would be a monstrous insult. Another option was to tell her he didn't want to discuss the subject but then she'd be hurt and he didn't want to hurt her. She also opened to him last night; didn't he owe her the same courtesy?

He could give her part of the story; he didn't have to tell her everything.

"I dream about Radd dying, about being left alone. It's a recurring dream, something I've been experiencing most of my life." He would not, *never*, tell her that he'd dreamed about her dying too. There were some things she didn't need to know.

Her hand came to rest on his thigh, her gentle squeeze suggesting support. "Oh, Digby, that's horrible."

She had no damn idea. "I'm sorry if I woke you," Digby muttered, glad his cap was still covering his eyes.

"I don't care about that. Have you told Radd about your nightmares?"

Now why would he do that? "Uh...*no*."

"You should. It helps to verbalize fears—it makes them smaller, weaker," Bay told him, her voice empathetic.

Before he could tell her that he'd rather have his toenails pulled off with rusty pliers, Olivia sat down on his stomach and he released a pained, "Oof." Despite having a little wind knocked out of him, he was incredibly grateful for her interruption. He couldn't think of a subject he'd less like to discuss.

Olivia swung one leg over him so that her chubby knees were on either side of his ribs and her feet in the sand. She lifted his cap off his face, stared down at him and pursed her lips. "Is Mommy Bay your girlfriend?"

Digby sent her a "help me" look, but Bay seemed like she was enjoying this interrogation far too much to put a stop to it. "Bay is my friend and a girl."

Bay smiled at his triumphant dodged-a-bullet expression.

"So she isn't your girlfriend," Liv stated.

He was being put on the spot by a three-year-old. This time Bay did come to his rescue. "Stop bugging Dig, Olivia."

Olivia threw her hands up in the air. "I was just asking a question!"

Bay sighed. "Digby and I are friends, Olivia."

"Oh. I understand."

"You do?" Digby asked the little girl.

"You can't be her boyfriend 'cause Mommy Bay is too pretty for you."

Digby turned to look at Bay who was, rather unsuccessfully, trying to hide her laughter. "I might never recover from this emotional damage, Adair."

"And she's only three. Imagine how savage she is going to be when she's sixteen," Bay told him, patting his hand.

Liv took his cap off his head and put it on hers. It immediately fell over her eyes and half her face. Digby took it off her and, ignoring her squawk of annoyance, tightened the band and put it back on her head. It was still too big but didn't completely cover her suck-you-in eyes.

Digby looked at Olivia and rested his hand on her chubby thigh. She was dressed in a little rash vest and matching shorts, designed to keep her from burning. In his cap, she looked too cute for words and his heart stumbled and banged off his chest.

"Here you go, sweetie." Bay handed Olivia her cup filled with weak, unsweetened tea. Leaning to the side, she placed her lips on Olivia's, who happily accepted her affectionate gesture. "Love you, baby girl."

"Love you more," Olivia automatically replied, telling Digby it was an oft-repeated phrase.

How could Bay's parents want to split these two up? Okay, Bay wasn't her biological mother but damn, she loved her niece with everything she had. Olivia was her entire world and Digby felt a pang of jealousy deep in his heart. He was, he reluctantly admitted, jealous that he'd never had a mother who loved him like that…

He felt stupid for wanting a moment that was long gone…

But he was damned if he'd let Olivia and Bay be separated. If the judge didn't rule in her favor in the custody battle, he'd contact his lawyers and he'd find out what he could

do to ensure that Bay and Olivia stayed together, that she became Olivia's mommy in
all the ways that counted.

He had wealth and power and he had no
problem using both to get the outcome he
wanted...

Digby yawned and lifted his hand to cover
his mouth. Despite making love to Bay quite a
few times, he'd slept like a rock. No, he'd only
thought he'd slept well because he couldn't
remember the dream that woke Bay up.

Damn, would he ever be free of them? And
he still hadn't managed to shake the memory
of the very weird dream he had of Bay taking
Radd's place in that coffin. Digby shuddered
and his skin turned to gooseflesh.

"I knows what I'm going to be when I grows
up," Olivia announced, her sweet voice the
distraction he needed. Under the bill of her
cap, her eyes radiated determination.

"Really?" Digby asked, sitting up but holding on to Olivia so that she stayed on his lap.
"What are you going to be? A doctor? A sci-
entist? An astronaut?"

Olivia looked at him like he'd grown two
heads. "No, silly."

"What are you going to be when you grow up, Liv?" Bay asked her, leaning back on her elbows, her long body sporting four bright pink triangles. Digby's glance went to her stomach and he stared at her belly ring, remembering the way his tongue swirled around that small, sexy indentation. And those long, shapely, stunning legs had wrapped around his hips...

Right, couldn't think of that right now. Mustn't think of anything they did until they were alone...

"I'm going to be a penguin."

"Huh?" Digby asked, having lost track of the conversation.

Olivia sent him a "keep up" look. "When I grows up, Digby, I'm going to be a penguin."

"Good plan," Digby told her, unable to hold back his grin. Man, he loved this kid. He surged to his feet and tucked her under his arm like a rugby ball. "And do you know what penguins must do?"

"What?" Liv squealed as he headed to the surf.

"They must swim and catch fish!" Digby

yelled, charging into the surf and releasing a banshee-like cry.

Olivia, being a warrior herself, did her best to outyell him.

Bay, he noticed when he looked back, just grinned before rolling onto her stomach and burying her nose in her book.

CHAPTER NINE

ON TUESDAY MORNING, back in Cape Town, Digby woke up feeling anxious and unsettled. After a long swim that failed to clear his head, he went into Green Point and the exclusive offices of Mabaso, Gumede and Klein, the lawyers dealing with his parents' estate.

It was also the day Bay would appear in court, fighting to keep Olivia. God, he wished he could be with her, giving her moral support, but his presence might harm her chances rather than help. It was a comfort to know that Mama B would be with her, as well as other members of the Samsodien family. Olivia would be in court as well and he hoped that she was too young to understand why she was there and what they were discussing.

But, because he needed Bay to know that he was thinking about her, he sent her a text message.

I'll be thinking of, and rooting for, you today. I know that the judge will make the right decision because you are what's best for Liv. You're a fantastic mom, sweetheart.

Call me as soon as it's over—I want to know how it went. Thanks for one of the best weekends of my life...

Digby turned his phone onto Silent and put it into the inner pocket of his suit jacket. Today was the day he and Radd were meeting the heir to their parents' fortune and, frankly, there were a million things he'd rather be doing today. Sure, it would be great to see Radd—he and Brin flew in late last night— but he had a million things to do and not much time to do them in.

He'd had a great weekend with Bay and Olivia but taking that time meant that he'd be working fourteen-hour days for the rest of the week to catch up. And to keep up that hectic pace, he needed to sleep, and last night, his nightmares returned with a vicious twist.

He'd dreamed, once again, of losing Radd. Then if that wasn't enough, when he finally fell asleep again, it was Bay's face in that black coffin.

He'd woken up tangled up in his sheets, his face and body wet with perspiration and his heart thundering, his arms reaching for Bay. When he realized where he was, alone in his own bed, and that he was having a nightmare, he felt nausea in the back of his throat and just—but only just—made it to the bathroom to throw up.

His nightmares, Digby decided as he entered the swish offices, were getting worse. Throughout his teens and twenties, they'd been vivid but short and he always managed to brush them from his mind. But these latest dreams were more terrors than nightmares and their negativity tended to be more long lasting, leaving him feeling unsettled and uptight for most of the day.

Digby strode up to the reception desk and handed the cool blonde a tight smile. "Tempest-Vane for Siya Mabaso, at nine o'clock."

"Nice to see you too, bro."

Digby turned around to see his brother standing behind him, casually dressed in an untucked, button-down shirt, chino shorts and loafers. Radd looked relaxed and happy, his dark blue eyes content.

Digby gripped his hand and pulled him into a hug. "Radd! Hell, I didn't even see you standing there."

"I noticed. Bit preoccupied, Dig?" Radd asked on an easy grin.

Just a bit. Mostly with a slim brunette with eyes the color of his favorite alcoholic drink. God help him.

"It's good to see you," Digby said. And it was. He and Radd had always been a team and they were stronger, and better, together. "How's Brin?"

"I left her in bed," Radd told him with a self-satisfied smile. "Though she is planning to get back to her shop today. She's feeling incredibly guilty for being away so long. She's wanting to open in six weeks."

Despite being engaged to one of the wealthiest people in the country, his future sister-in-law still wanted to pursue a career in floral design. Digby admired her for following her dream and kudos to his big brother for allowing her to fly.

Radd placed a hand on his shoulder and

nodded to the sharply dressed lawyer waiting for them across the room. "You ready for this?"

Digby shrugged. "I guess. Though why this person wants to meet us, I have no damn idea."

"Let's go find out," Radd suggested.

Digby buttoned his suit jacket and followed his casually dressed brother into a conference room, wondering why his heart was thundering. There was nothing to be concerned about—his parents' heir had no connection to them, couldn't hurt them.

He was just here to satisfy his curiosity; that was all.

Then why did he feel like he did this morning when he woke after that nightmare? Shivery and sick, feeling like everything had changed.

Digby took a deep breath and greeted Siya Mabaso, shaking his hand before looking around the small conference room. In the corner, by the window, stood a familiar figure and Digby blinked, convinced he was seeing a mirage, that she was an illusion.

"Roisin?" he asked, not caring that his voice

was cracking. "What the hell are you doing here?"

"Radd, Digby, meet Roisin O'Keefe. Your sister."

Digby left the meeting feeling shell-shocked and disorientated. Siya explained that Roisin was born in the States when he was ten—that explained Gil and Zia's long absence that year—and that her adoption had been facilitated by a lawyer in the States. His parents must've realized that their fourth child was a girl and, knowing they wouldn't get a pay-out from the trust for not producing another boy child, decided to dump their unwanted daughter.

God, it physically hurt that he was related to them.

Thankfully, Roisin hit the jackpot with her adopted parents; the O'Keefes were a wealthy, childless couple who adored their adopted daughter.

Apparently, both Roisin and her parents had been shocked to discover that she was the biological daughter of two of the most notorious socialites in Africa and the heir to an estate worth billions.

As an only child, she'd explained, she'd always wanted siblings but she understood that, given their fame, news that there was another Tempest-Vane sibling would be explosive. Her dropping into Radd's and Digby's lives would set the tabloids on fire. And, she candidly admitted, she wanted to meet Radd and Digby first, to decide whether they were the type of people she wanted to know.

If she liked them, fine, if not, her identity could forever remain a secret.

Apparently, she liked them. Well, she liked Digby. *Hoo-bloody-rah.*

Digby, flying down Chapman's Peak on his Ducati, felt the power between his legs and gave his superbike more force, feeling his heart rate kick up a notch as adrenaline coursed through his system.

He had a sister, another sibling, God help him. He was furious that she'd lied to him, that she'd sought employment at The Vane to push herself into his life, into his world. He'd employed her to look after Olivia, had trusted her with his lover's child, with the little person he was crazy about.

Yet he hadn't known whom she was or her true agenda.

He felt like a bloody fool.

He needed to tell Bay, needed her to know that Roisin wasn't whom she said she was, that she'd been lying to him, them. But he couldn't talk to Bay, not yet.

Not until he got his head on straight.

Up until six weeks ago, he'd been happy in his single life, content to have only his brother to worry about. But now he had a sister, a sister-in-law, a lover and his lover's kid, all clamoring for a piece of his soul.

He couldn't do it. Radd was the only family Digby had, all he needed.

It was bad enough that he lived in constant fear of losing his brother but now he was also dreaming about Bay, and obviously, he was worried about losing her too. What was next, him perpetually fretting about losing her, losing Liv? Would that worry extend to Roisin, to Brin?

He couldn't do it; he didn't want the additional emotional stress. There were suddenly too many people in his life and he couldn't, wouldn't give them the power to hijack his heart. No, he preferred to fly solo, thank you very much.

He couldn't get rid of Radd, and he didn't want to. And Brin was part of his life. But he didn't have to engage with Roisin, he didn't need a sister.

As for Bay, well, it was time to let her go. It would hurt, for a little while, but she was a risk he couldn't take. Didn't want to take. From tonight, from *now*, he was going to revert to his old life, to what he knew, to what he was good at. Casual flings, ships-in-the-night relationships, nothing that involved any risk.

Digby whipped into a turnout, kicked down his stand and switched off the engine. Taking off his helmet, he stared down to the sea kissing the rocks below and tried not to remember Bay and Olivia poking around the rock pools in Mozambique. He pushed the memory away. He'd miss them but it was better this way.

After pulling out his phone, he grimaced at the many, many missed calls—Bay, Radd and Roisin—and switched to his text-messaging app.

There were twenty, twenty-five messages, and he again ignored the ones from Radd and Roisin. But he couldn't resist opening the first of Bay's many texts.

The judge decided not to wait and made his ruling immediately! I'm officially Liv's mommy! Want to celebrate with me tonight?

Dig, I can't get a hold of you. Call me.

Digby, I really need to talk to you...

Dig, Roisin told me about today, that she's your sister. She really feels bad about lying to you, and she needs to talk to you. I need to talk to you. Call me, please.

Dig, it's been hours and hours. I'm really worried.

She didn't need to worry; he hadn't asked her to. He'd been looking after himself for a long, long time and he was fine. He didn't need her sympathy or her company, to help him work his way through this mess.

They were over…

They had to be.

Digby slapped his helmet back onto his head and revved his bike, spinning it in a tight circle to face the road. Giving the bike power, he shot away and his speed quickly climbed, then climbed some more. His heart sat in his throat as he flung the bike around the tight corners and adrenaline pumped through his body.

If he could only go fast enough to forget.

Have just heard that D used his private entrance ten minutes ago. Go kick his ass.

In the ballroom of The Vane, Bay read Roisin's message once, then again. She quickly typed her reply.

How do you know?

I made friends with one of the guys manning the security cameras. Roisin's message popped onto her screen seconds later. Let me know how it goes.

Bay looked at her computer screen and frowned at the open tabs on it.

How to Cope After a Breakup
Steps to Treating the Pain of a Breakup
How to Heal Fast After Your Heart Has
Been Broken

Stupid internet and its super-stupid advice.

She needed a fall-out-of-love pill, something to erase everything she felt, to help her forget the possibilities of the amazing life they could have had together. Her vision for her future coalesced nine days ago when she'd seen the judge give his surprising verdict, shortly after he heard all the evidence around why she should keep custody of Olivia.

The judge said nice things: that anyone could see that she and Liv were a family and that they were a tight unit. It was a pity that there wasn't a father figure in Liv's life. He was concerned about the animosity between her and her parents but it wasn't a reason to deny her custody.

Maybe they could work it out, the judge suggested, before awarding her permanent custody there and then.

Instead of reacting jubilantly, Bay, her arms

around Liv's little waist, buried her face in the child's hair, biting her own lip to stop herself from yelling that Liv did have a father figure in her life, a man they both adored. A man she was completely, thoroughly, impossibly in love with.

But, because he was currently running away from reality, from a situation he no longer had control over, she was alone.

She shouldn't be alone. Neither of them should. They were better, stronger, together.

Bay shut down her laptop, thinking that Digby was taking a long time to reach the same conclusion. And, she reminded herself, he might never get to that point. *You can't force people to love you the way you need to be loved, Bay, you know this.*

Love meant different things to different people: to her father, it was control, to Digby it represented fear and loss.

Either way, both the men she'd loved most in her life had taken her love, then dismissed her and left her swinging in the wind.

Damn them.

She might not be able to stop the people she loved from treating her like she was disposable but that didn't mean they could get away with it.

After walking out of the ballroom, Bay used the staff passages to avoid the guests and finally emerged at the back of the hotel. As she walked to Digby's house, the many reasons she was angry with him tumbled through her head.

In ten days, he never once called or even replied to her many, many messages. Not even to congratulate or acknowledge her winning the custody battle for Liv. He'd gone completely silent and it was no comfort to know that he wasn't talking to his brand-new sister, or apparently, as she'd heard from Roisin, to Radd either.

But while he wasn't talking to his brother, his new sister or to her, he hadn't been alone. The tabloid press had been ecstatic about his return to the clubbing and partying scene and there had been photos in the gossip columns every day this week. He'd attended many, many parties and he'd only left the clubs when they finally closed, usually accompanied by a stacked blonde. He'd run up Table Mountain, gone skydiving and free dived

with sharks off Hermanus. He'd also managed to rack up a slew of speeding tickets in
six days from pushing his Ducati to higher
and higher speeds.

Wild Digby Tempest-Vane was back with a
vengeance and the press was salivating.

Bay just wanted to bash his head in.

How dare he? How dare he act like she and
Liv, Roisin and Radd, didn't matter? That
they weren't important enough to let them
know that he was okay? They'd had such a
marvelous weekend away in Mozambique
and Bay thought they were on the path to
creating something special. He'd been sweet
and considerate and seemed to enjoy spending time with not only her but Liv. She'd tried
not to, but she'd started to think, just a little,
that they had a chance of a relationship, of
something permanent.

What a colossal fool she'd been. From the
beginning, she'd known he was going to
hurt her and she wasn't surprised by that.
Although she'd never expected him to disappear, to break contact with everyone who
loved him.

But someone needed to tell him his behavior was unacceptable and inexcusable. She could, just, cope with him hurting her, but she refused to condone his behavior toward Roisin.

Bay didn't bother to knock; she just stormed into his house, shouting his name. He emerged from his study, his eyes flat and his face pale. Bay put her hand on her heart and shook her head at his gaunt cheeks, his red-rimmed eyes. "Wow, looking good, Tempest-Vane."

"If you are going to be sarcastic you can just bugger off," Digby told her, walking past her to head for the kitchen. He fiddled with the coffee machine, keeping his back to her. "Actually, just go, Bay. We have nothing to say to each other."

Bay felt a red-hot surge of anger. "You might not have anything to say to me but I have a hell of a lot to say to you!"

Digby turned to face her, his hands gripping the counter behind him. "Get on with it then—I have somewhere to be."

She wasn't going to ask; she wasn't going to be *that* woman. "Who is she today? Do you even know her name?"

Really, Bay, why are you asking questions

you really, really don't want to know the answer to? What is wrong with you?

Digby met her eyes and for a second, maybe less, she saw shame in his eyes. Then it disappeared and he handed her a laconic shrug. "I just call them sweetheart, they seem to like that."

Just like she had. Bay sent him a hard look and shook her head. She didn't believe him. He was bullshitting her. Yeah, she could easily believe that he'd been clubbing and doing all those other crazy things, but she knew he hadn't been with another woman.

He was being a jerk, but she knew him... He wouldn't jump from her bed to someone else's. He might've been on a tear this week, but she could see how much pain he was in; it was there in his churning eyes, in his too-tight lips, reflected in the fact that his shoulders were halfway to his ears.

She'd learned to read him and could feel the confusion and hurt rolling off him in hot waves. He didn't want to deal with the idea of having more family; he simply couldn't bear it. He'd trained himself to keep isolated, to not allow any love into his life. He already worried about losing his brother, and the idea of having a sister had, she was sure, rocked his world. Digby's biggest fear was loving and losing someone he loved, and having someone new in his life freaked him out.

And adding her and Liv to the equation was a sure way to make him panic and want to run.

"Talk to me, Dig," she said, her anger dying and sadness rising.

"Nothing to say." Digby whipped out the stinging words.

"So, you're quite fine with the fact that you have a sister?"

"We might share some genes but, as far as I'm concerned, she's just another Tempest-Vane employee. I don't intend to have any-thing to do with her," Digby said, his voice flat. But longing crossed his face and Bay knew he was lying through his teeth. "Radd is my family, my only family."

Every time he said that it hurt a little more. But she couldn't think of herself, she had to concentrate on trying to get Digby to move off the I'm-better-alone hill he was currently defending. Not for her but for Roisin, whom she adored and who wanted to have a relationship with her biological brother.

But mostly she wanted this for Digby. She understood that Roisin's revelation was a lot for him to come to terms with, that her coming into his life was too much for him to deal with...

But Bay understood that Digby needed more people in his life who loved him. Family was a precious gift and not something to be easily dismissed. And family wasn't confined to people with whom one shared DNA; after all, it had been Mama B who held her hand during the custody battle, Mama B who led her and Olivia from the courtroom after the verdict.

It was Mama B who held her as she watched her parents walk away from their granddaughter without a word. Mama B remained in her life as her parents walked out of it.

Family wasn't something to be so easily dismissed, Bay thought. Especially when that family was walking toward you. When they didn't want anything from you but to be part of your life and, if you were brave enough, to love you.

"You are the reason why Roisin decided to come clean—she feels a connection to you," Bay persisted.

"I. Don't. Care," Digby said, through gritted teeth.

Bay folded her arms across her chest and looked him in the eye. "This is all pretty overwhelming, isn't it? You've fallen for me, and Liv, you have a new sister, Radd is engaged to Brin... For a guy who's always felt alone, being surrounded by people who want a piece of you must be disconcerting."

"I haven't fallen for you," Digby muttered, his tone harsh.

Oh, he so had. "You told me once that you craved attention and that you looked for it everywhere, that it fueled so many of your actions. Funny that now that you have a bunch of attention, from people who claim to love you, who want to spend their lives loving you, you are running from it. What's up with that, Dig?"

"Will you please *go*?"

Not yet. Bay decided to push him some more. "Wait, I'm trying to understand this. So, you are happy to have the attention of strangers and the press and acquaintances, but you bolt when you are faced with real love, true love?"

Digby stared at a point past her shoulder. "Bay, I am tired and pissed off and I'm done with this conversation. Will you please leave?"

He roared the last sentence and Bay forced herself not to react, to keep her expression bland. He didn't scare her; he never would.

"I'll go, in a minute. I just have a few things to say first," Bay said, her heart and stomach doing backflips.

"Get on with it," Digby growled.

Bay was desperate to get through to him but knew she would only have one shot at this. She considered and discarded a couple of sentences and when Digby threw up his hands in annoyance at having to wait, she allowed the words to flow.

"I love you, Digby."

And she always would. Sure, she'd been on the receiving end of conditional love but that didn't mean she had to give it. She knew, somewhere deep in her soul where truth resided, that if Digby was capable of giving her what she needed, he would. He wasn't doing this to hurt her, but because he'd been hurt, time and time again, by people and circumstances.

"I know that's not something you want to hear but it's something I want you to know." She saw him jerk, clocked his deep frown. He wasn't happy to hear her declaration and, knowing she had nothing more to lose, she carried on.

"Someday, I hope you realize that we could have something pretty wonderful," Bay calmly stated. "But, if you decide that you want us, you'd better be prepared to give me what *I* want, Tempest-Vane."

He lifted his chin, those blue eyes blazing. Digby didn't like ultimatums; he far preferred to give them. Too damn bad.

She refused to be intimidated by him. "I know what it's like to live with uncertainty, what it's like to live with someone who is exceptionally good at giving and then withdrawing affection. I refuse to love someone like that again. In Mozambique, you gave Liv, and me, your love and affection but, the next day, you withdrew it and dropped out of our lives. That is not acceptable behavior."

Bay pushed a weary hand through her hair. "If you come back to me, you'd better be damn sure that I, and Liv, are a priority and not an option. We'd better be the most important people in your life because I won't settle for anything less, for her or for me. If you come back, you'd better be prepared to commit to me, and to Liv, in every way that matters. Are you hearing me on this, Digby?"

Resentment flashed in his eyes. "You want me to be Olivia's dad."

She did, so she nodded. She refused to settle for anything less than everything, for even a fraction less than wonderful. "Yeah, I do. You're living in fear, Digby, and I wish you'd realize that none of us is out to hurt you.

"If you take a chance on me, I promise I will always be there for you, that I will never willingly walk away. Apart from infidelity and abuse, neither of which are in your nature, the only way you will lose me, and Olivia, is by not letting us in. I won't abandon you. Neither will your family—you just have to give them, *us*, a chance."

She'd said a lot already; she might as well get it all out. "But I also need to be able to rely on you, to know that you are not going to freak out and run when life throws us a curveball. I want to know that I can rely on you when things get tough, to celebrate with me when things go well. You have no idea how much you hurt me by not acknowledging my winning custody of Liv. I needed to share that with you but you weren't there for me. I was, *am*, gutted about that."

Desperation and guilt flared in his eyes but Bay forced herself to ignore what she saw. "I'm also so sad that you didn't come to me when you heard about Roisin. I could've helped you make sense of it but you ran and looked for attention from people who don't matter.

"I matter, Digby. So does your family." Bay lifted her fingers to her cheeks, cursing her tears. She lifted her hands as Digby took a step toward her and she violently shook her head.

She had to end this conversation before she lost it completely and broke down in front of him.

Finding the last of her courage, she looked at Digby, his image blurry through her tears. "Make damn sure you know what you want before you come back, Tempest-Vane. And if you don't, no hard feelings. I found a way to live without my dad's love—I will do the same with you too."

Feeling a little broken, and a lot sad, Bay turned away from him and stumbled toward the door, frantically wiping her tears away.

He'd come to her or he wouldn't. There was nothing more she could do.

Because he'd slammed down a bottle of whiskey—alone—after Bay left him, and was the architect of his own massive headache, Digby decided that he didn't deserve painkillers.

He was regretting that decision as he walked down the path leading from his house to the hotel. The sun felt like a million acid-tipped needles digging into his eyeballs and he was fairly sure his head was going to drop off his shoulders at any second.

I promise I will always be there for you, that I will never willingly walk away.

You're living in fear.

I wish you'd realize that none of us is out to hurt you.

Yeah, the pain was nothing he didn't deserve.

Digby sighed and rubbed the back of his neck. After a long night and a great deal of self-examination, recriminations and kicking his own ass, he knew he had fences to mend, explanations and decisions to make. He didn't want to do any of it...dealing with people he loved was exhausting. It was easier to pretend when he was amongst strangers. And that was why he'd run from Roisin, from Radd and yeah, from Bay.

Strangers didn't ask questions, demand more, couldn't force him to confront feelings he wasn't ready to deal with. And when he was chasing adrenaline, he had to—his life depended on it—push everything else away and focus on the task at hand. If he didn't, he could die.

He didn't want to die, but God, he wouldn't mind it if someone cut off his head to get rid of his headache.

First things first...

Standing on the edge of the white-to-pink-to-red rose garden, Digby pulled out his phone and called Radd. His brother answered on the third ring. "You alive?" Radd asked, sounding tense.

"Yeah."

Radd didn't speak again and Digby sighed. Radd wasn't going to make this easy for him; none of them, damn them, would. "So much happened very quickly."

It was a weak excuse but the only one he was prepared to give. "Yeah, I heard that you fell in love around the same time you heard about Roisin," Radd commented, his voice bland.

Digby dropped his phone to look at his screen. Shaking his head, he lifted it up to his ear again. "I don't know that I'm in love with her, Radd."

"Of course you are, Dig. Any idiot, apparently, can see it," Radd told him, sounding impatient. "I really like her, by the way, so does Brin. Roisin considers her to be a very good friend."

He couldn't think of Bay, not just yet. He needed to get his family situation sorted and then he'd deal with these churning, burning, crazy feelings he had for Bay.

"What does Roisin want from us, Radd?"

"Why don't you ask her yourself?" Radd asked. "And when you're done with that, pull your head out of your ass and go and talk to Bay."

Frank, older-brother advice. Not that it was needed; he was planning to do that. He didn't know if she'd accept his apology but he had to try, dammit.

But, before he ended this conversation, he needed to say one thing, just one, to Radd. Digby felt his throat tightening and pushed the words up his throat. "Radd, just don't..." his voice, to his dismay, cracked.

"Dig? Don't what?" Radd asked, immediately sounding concerned.

Digby ran his hand over his eyes, cursing the burn he felt within them. "Bay said that I should tell you that I've had nightmares about you most of my life, well, since Jack died. I dream that I'm burying you, saying goodbye..."

He shoved the words past the massive ball

in his too-tight throat. "Anyway, I can't lose you so don't die on me, okay?"

Radd was silent for a long time before Digby heard his heavy sigh. "Dig, I have a life partner I love and adore—I want to have kids as soon as we can. I want my brother, and my new sister, to be an integral part of my life going forward. I have no intention of going anywhere."

He couldn't respond, too choked up to speak. But he did feel a little lighter for voicing his biggest fear.

"Dig?"

"Yeah, I'm here."

"You've got fences to mend, apologies to make, a ton-load of groveling to do if you want to win Bay back."

"Thank you, Captain Obvious," Digby told him. Then he sighed. "But hell, you're not wrong. Any advice on how to grovel? If I recall, you had to do it with Brin…"

"I did not grovel. I explained my position," Radd growled.

"Brin says you groveled and I believe her," Digby teased him, needing to distance himself from the emotion swirling between them.

He started to walk again, heading toward the childcare center on the western edge of the property.

"Bloody hell, you're annoying," Radd retorted before disconnecting. Digby's smile faded as he put his hand on the door leading to the building he'd erected to entertain the guests' smaller kids. Roisin would be inside, as well as Liv.

Two of the three females causing havoc in his life...

Olivia was the first to see him and she let out a high-pitched squeal before bounding over to him, all but flying by the time she reached him. He scooped her up and closed his eyes when he felt her little face in his neck, all doubts about what he wanted fading.

He wanted to be Olivia's dad, to be Bay's husband, to spend the rest of his life loving them, and any other children they had, with everything he had.

Liv was the first to pull back and she placed her tiny hands on his cheeks, before dropping a kiss on his lips. "I's missed you."

Digby's heart skipped a beat at her shy declaration. "I missed you too, kiddo."

"I know." Liv narrowed her amazing eyes at him. "Are you going to buy me a present because you missed me?"

Digby didn't bother to hide his grin. She was smart little baggage and she'd keep him, God willing, on his toes and wrapped around her already overdeveloped finger for the rest of his life. "What do you want?"

"I still wants an elephant and a penguin."

Digby dropped a kiss on her nose. "Mmm, what if I bought you a stuffed elephant and penguin instead?"

"Like Fluffy?" Liv, her hands still on his cheeks, considered his offer. "I'll think about it. I's go play now."

She pushed against his hold and Digby lowered her to the ground, watching as she scampered off to join a little boy playing with blocks across the room. There, he thought, went part of his heart.

"She's a handful but so, so sweet."

Digby turned at the voice behind him and saw Roisin leaning against the wall, her blue eyes wary. She had his eyes, he noticed, Radd's chin, their height. With her dark hair and blue eyes, she was, absolutely, a Tempest-

Vane and Digby couldn't believe he hadn't noticed it before.

"Hey," he said, wincing at the inane comment.

"Hey back," Roisin said, her arms crossing over her chest as if to protect her heart. He'd hurt her, he realized, just as he'd hurt Bay. *Enough of that now, Tempest-Vane.*

Going with his gut, Digby opened his arms and waited, with bated breath, to find out whether Roisin would accept his gesture. She sniffled, just once, before moving toward him, then hugging him tightly.

"I didn't mean to deceive you, Dig. I just wanted to go slow," she muttered against his chest.

Digby ran his hand down her long braid. "It's okay, Ro. And can I say, although it's a bit late…welcome to our dysfunctional family."

Roisin stood back and wiped her tears away with the balls of her hands. Then she covered her eyes with her hands. "I needed time to see if you were anything like your, *our*, parents. If you were, I was going to fade away, not make contact."

"Smart girl," Digby replied. Hell, in her position, he would've done exactly the same thing. After leading her outside, Digby pushed her into one of the two chairs on the veranda and sat down on the opposite one.

Roisin sniffed and pulled a tissue out of her pocket. After blowing her nose, she tried to smile. "I was only told about the inheritance when your parents died. I didn't know about them before. I was shocked at suddenly becoming an heiress."

"I bet."

"But they, according to the lawyer, kept track of me," Roisin stated. Then determination burned in the eyes that met his. "I told Radd and I'm telling you, I don't want everything they left me. I want you two to choose anything you want and I'll auction everything else."

"I don't want anything," Digby said, placing his hand on her knee. "I have everything I need."

"Radd said the same thing," Roisin replied. "But there are some boxes of jewelry, photos and knickknacks you may want. I think it might be your grandparents' stuff—it's pretty old. Maybe you'd like to look through that, at least."

"I'd like that," Digby told her. "But sell the rest, Roisin, bank the proceeds."

"They left me enough cash for several life-times and I don't need that much money. I thought that I could donate the money raised at the auction to the Tempest-Vane founda-tion. Anonymously, of course."

They'd be grateful but it wasn't necessary, he told her. And that raised another point. "Do you want a public acknowledgment from us, Ro?"

Roisin cocked her head. "Would you give me one?"

Of that he had no doubt; he'd be proud to call her his sister. "Absolutely. It will create a firestorm in the media, but if that's what you want, then sure."

Roisin placed her hand on her chest. "You and Radd are amazing and I'm so lucky to have found you. But no, I'd prefer to avoid the press. But thank you for the offer."

Digby shrugged. "You're our sister." He heard someone calling her name and Roisin checked her watch. "It's outside playtime—I need to go," she explained as she stood up.

As if they'd been doing it forever, she stepped into his arms again for another hug. When she pulled back, he asked another question. "Why are you still working? I mean, now that we know who you are, you no longer need to pretend."

Roisin sent him a sweet smile. "I like to work and I love kids. And my friend needed me to look after her little girl."

Digby looked down at his feet, noticing a new rip in the knee of his oldest jeans. "How is she?" he quietly asked.

"Sad. But strong," Roisin replied. "Missing you. She's in the ballroom if you are looking for her."

He was. Honestly, he'd been looking for her all his life but never knew it.

CHAPTER TEN

BAY, SITTING ON the floor in the corner of the ballroom, lifted her head up from her sketch pad to look around the space. It was the lack of noise that first caught her attention and, yep, the room was completely empty.

She looked at her watch and frowned. It wasn't tea or lunchtime. The renovation crew should still be working; this room had to be finished in time for the Table Mountain Ball in a few weeks.

Where was everybody?

"Do you know the definition of the Greek word *philophobia*?"

Bay's head whipped in the direction of Digby's voice and eventually found him, standing next to the French doors, the sun creating a halo around his head. She almost snorted; Digby was as far from an angel as anyone could be and she far preferred naughty to nice anyway. Wearing a white linen shirt, sleeves rolled up his forearms, and ripped and battered designer jeans, flip-flops on his feet, he looked hot and sexy and hot...

She was repeating herself.

Annoyed by her instinctive, uncontrollable response to him, Bay scowled. "Did you come here to slow down work—" she looked around the ballroom, realizing he was the only person who could clear the room so fast "—or to torment me with the meaning of obscure Greek words?"

Digby walked into the ballroom, across to where she sat, and sank to the floor in front of her before crossing his legs and placing his elbows on his knees. "It originates from two Greek words: *philos* which means loving, and *phobos* which means fear. I've been suffering from the fear of love all my life."

Bay bit her lip, wondering where he was going with this.

"I'm terrified of love, having it, dealing with it, losing it. It's easier to dismiss it, to tell yourself you didn't want it in the first place."

Bay rested the back of her head against the wall behind her and waited for him to continue.

"Then you dropped into my life and made me confront that fear," Digby told her, sounding a little cross. "I was just wrapping my head around *that* notion when I found out that Roisin is my sister, and I, sort of, lost it."

"Really? Sort of?" Bay sarcastically replied.

Digby pulled her sketch pad from her grip and looked down at what she'd been drawing. Bay started to blush as he inspected her sketch of him. She should've been working but, feeling sad and dispirited, she'd sat down in the corner, and when her thoughts went to Digby she'd started to sketch his likeness. Her sketch looked a lot like him, she thought. Complete with tired eyes and gaunt cheeks.

"Liv's right—I'm definitely not pretty enough for you."

Bay forced herself to speak. "I don't want pretty, Digby. I want real."

Digby slowly nodded. "Okay, how is this for real?" He hesitated and Bay held her breath, knowing he was about to say something momentous. "Except for Radd, I've been on my own for a long, long time. I've liked being on my own—I've loved my freedom. I've had no one to answer to.

"Over the last couple of weeks, I've met you, I've met Liv and I've met Roisin and each of you, in different ways, has taken—despite my objections—a piece of my heart. The tiny piece that's left, that's mine alone, is terrified that I will never get those pieces back." Digby looked at her, his eyes deep, dark and intense. "I'm scared, Bay. Can you understand that? You're each offering something I desperately want, but history has taught me that I don't get the things I most want."

"Like your parents' love and attention," Bay murmured.

"And the love I did have, the love I relied on more than I realized, went away when Jack died. Love, to me, is synonymous with loss, constant disappointment and unfulfillment."

Oh, God, when he put it like that, she saw the uphill climb she'd asked him to make and accepted that she'd asked for too much. He wouldn't be able to love her the way she needed him to. She'd asked for far too much.

"Let's just stop here, Digby—I can't do

this," she said, her words running together. "I understand why you are hesitant to get involved but I can't be anything *but* involved. I can't be the one giving everything and not getting what I need."

She wouldn't cry; she wouldn't! She'd stand up, hold her head up high and walk out of the room. "I'll leave all my designs for the next designer and I'll get out of your hair. I'd still really appreciate a letter of recommendation if you wouldn't mind giving me one."

Bay tried to stand up but Digby's strong hand on her leg kept her in place. "I have no intention of writing a letter of recommendation because I am not letting you go. After you finish the designs for The Vane, I need you to redesign some of the suites at the resort in Bazaruto—I've decided to purchase that place. Oh, you'd also need to decorate our new house."

"What new house?" Bay asked, utterly confused. "What are you talking about?"

"Well, the barn isn't suitable—Liv is too young to negotiate the walkway and those stairs. And, while I love your cottage, baby, it's a bit small for all three of us." His lips quirked into that sexy smile she loved so much. "And the elephants and penguins Liv is insisting I buy for her."

"What?"

"Hopefully, she's resigned to having stuffed animals but, because she's a tough negotiator and I can't seem to say no to her, who knows?"

Bay leaned forward, gripped his shirt and attempted to shake him. "Digby! What the hell are you talking about?"

Digby lifted his hand to stroke her face with his fingertips. "I'm still scared, Bay, but I'm more scared of living my life without you than I am of losing you. I love you so much, sweetheart."

"Uh…"

Was she really hearing what she was hearing? Or was she suffering from some sort of selective hearing?

"Would you mind repeating that?" she politely asked, pushing down on her chest to keep her heart from shoving through her skin.

"I love you. I love Liv," Digby told her, resting his forehead against hers. "Will you both be mine? For the rest of my life?"

Bay bit her bottom lip, blinking away her tears. Bay lifted her hand to his neck, needing to feel his warmth, his solidity. "Is this really happening?"

Digby looked around the ballroom and shrugged. "Not exactly where I thought I'd propose but…what the hell. So, what do you say, Bay?"

"To what?"

Digby smiled. "Wow, I'm really bad at this." He picked up her left hand and stroked her ring finger. "I'd like to put a ring on this finger, Bay. Because you don't seem to be grasping innuendo today, I want to put my ring on your finger, have your ring on mine. I want to marry you and I really, really hope you want to marry me."

Of course she wanted to marry him, to be his. "Are you sure, Digby?"

Digby nodded. "Very sure, sweetheart. Look, I accept that I am a bit of a mess, emotionally, and that I won't always get it right. But I promise to never run again, Bay. I promise to stick. And stay. I promise to work it out. And yeah, we'll fight but I promise that

I will never punish you by withdrawing my love. I never break my promises, Bay.

"I'm not the man I was yesterday, a month ago, six months ago. You've made me better, Bay. I promise to love you with everything I am, all that I've got."

Bay stared at him, overwhelmed by his declaration, feeling like her heart was on a wild ride. She saw worry jump into his eyes, then fear. When she didn't speak, she saw him retreating, the light fading from his eyes. "I'm too late, aren't I?"

He started to rise but Bay gripped his shirt in her fist, twisting the material in her hand. "*Yes.* Yes, Dig, to everything. The new house, the job, the penguins and elephants, but only of the stuffed variety. A huge, shiny, yes, please, to becoming your wife."

She heard, and felt, his relief-tinged laughter. Burying her face in his neck, she wound her arms around it and breathed him in. "I can't wait to be yours, Dig."

Digby's broad hand stroked her back. "You have been, from the moment I first saw you. It just took my brain a while to catch up with my heart."

"I'm so very glad it did," Bay told him, pulling back to look into his lovely, love-filled eyes. "I love you so much, darling."

Digby's mouth drifted across hers. "I love you more, Bay. I always will."

And at that moment, hearing the words she and Liv often exchanged, she knew that he was, absolutely, the third point in their triangle, the compass point they'd been missing. Liv's new dad. Her best friend. Her love and her life.

In his eyes, she saw everything she'd ever need.

* * * * *